Sudden Chaos

As the five gents sprang to their feet, clawing iron, Long-arm slammed his shot glass down on the bar and reached for the Winchester. He rammed a shell into the breech. "Hold on—federal law!"

The words had about as much effect on the hard cases as spit would have on a prairie twister.

They were all shouting now, drawing iron, aiming at the back of the room, where the black-haired gent was flop-ping around on the floor like a landed fish and the marshal was giving the table a final toss to his left.

A bull-necked, red-haired gent seemed to have the drop on the local badge-toter. Longarm snapped his rifle to his shoulder, aimed, and fired . . .

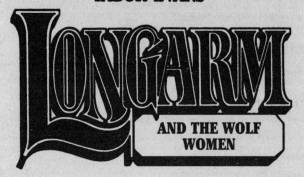

TABOR EVANS

LONGARM

AND THE WOLF WOMEN

JOVE BOOKS, NEW YORK

THE BERKLEY PUBLISHING GROUP
Published by the Penguin Group
Penguin Group (USA) Inc.
375 Hudson Street, New York, New York 10014, USA
Penguin Group (Canada), 90 Eglinton Avenue East, Suite 700, Toronto, Ontario M4P 2Y3, Canada
(a division of Pearson Penguin Canada Inc.)
Penguin Books Ltd., 80 Strand, London WC2R 0RL, England
Penguin Group Ireland, 25 St. Stephen's Green, Dublin 2, Ireland (a division of Penguin Books Ltd.)
Penguin Group (Australia), 250 Camberwell Road, Camberwell, Victoria 3124, Australia
(a division of Pearson Australia Group Pty. Ltd.)
Penguin Books India Pvt. Ltd., 11 Community Centre, Panchsheel Park, New Delhi—110 017, India
Penguin Group (NZ), 67 Apollo Drive, Mairangi Bay, Auckland 1311, New Zealand
(a division of Pearson New Zealand Ltd.)
Penguin Books (South Africa) (Pty.) Ltd., 24 Sturdee Avenue, Rosebank, Johannesburg 2196,
South Africa

Penguin Books Ltd., Registered Offices: 80 Strand, London WC2R 0RL, England

This is a work of fiction. Names, characters, places, and incidents either are the product of the author's imagination or are used fictitiously, and any resemblance to actual persons, living or dead, business establishments, events, or locales is entirely coincidental.

LONGARM AND THE WOLF WOMEN

A Jove Book / published by arrangement with the author

PRINTING HISTORY
Jove edition / April 2007

Copyright © 2007 by The Berkley Publishing Group.

ISBN: 978-0-515-14284-6

JOVE®
Jove Books are published by The Berkley Publishing Group,
a division of Penguin Group (USA) Inc.,
375 Hudson Street, New York, New York 10014.
JOVE is a registered trademark of Penguin Group (USA) Inc.
The "J" design is a trademark belonging to Penguin Group (USA) Inc.

PRINTED IN THE UNITED STATES OF AMERICA

10 9 8 7 6 5 4 3 2 1

Chapter 1

"What kind of woman would use her body to lure a man to his death?" asked the Diamondback grocer, Mike Baron.

He squatted beside a small coffee fire with two of his fellow townsmen and the young deputy U.S. marshal, Johnny Parsons. The men made up a posse tracking savage killers. "I mean, that just ain't right," Baron continued. "It's takin' . . . takin' . . ."

Baron cast his eyes about the coffee fire before him, as though searching for the right words.

"Unfair advantage?" the chubby Dutch harness maker, Jan Behunek, finished for him as he touched a smoldering stick to a freshly rolled cigarette.

"Yeah, that's what it is." Baron nodded vigorously. "It ain't right for a woman to hold a man's natural desires against him. No, sir. Those women need to be locked up for a good long time!"

"Hang 'em, I say," said Ned Miller, the livery barn owner and oldest member of the posse. "Right along with their old man. Just as soon as we catch 'em. What's good enough for the sire is good enough for his fillies!"

Miller turned to the red-haired, pug-nosed federal lawman, Johnny Parsons, who'd been sent to the little town of

Diamondback in northern Colorado to corral the kill-crazy mountain man, Magnus Magnusson, and the mountain man's equally crazy, albeit beautiful, daughters. They'd been on the threesome's trail for two days, following the Diamondback River through the long, serpentine gorge of Diamondback Canyon.

Parsons had secured the help of the three men because they'd found the bodies of the three soldiers Magnusson had slain last week, when they were heading back to Diamondback after a hunting trip, and could lead Parsons through the maze-like canyon to the site of the killings. One of the soldiers had lived a few hours after the townsmen found him, and had told a frightening story.

Now, just after noon of a warm spring day in the foothills of the Rocky Mountains, they'd stopped to boil coffee and to water their horses in the Diamondback River.

"What do you say, Deputy?" Miller asked. "You don't see any point in wastin' time haulin' that tribe in for a court trial, do you? They're cold-blooded killers! We seen what they done with our own eyes!"

Deputy U.S. Marshal Parsons held one of his matching, pearl-gripped .45s to his left ear as he slowly turned the cylinder, listening intently to each click. When he'd heard each of the six, satisfactory clicks, he lowered the revolver, twirled the gun in his right hand, and ran his left forefinger through his thin, red mustache, as if making sure it was still there.

"It don't matter, Mr. Miller." The young lawman looked across the fire at the livery owner, his one slightly crossed eye spoiling the authoritative stare he always strained for. "The law says we bring that gentleman and his two daughters to justice, and that's exactly what I aim to do. My boss, Marshal Billy Vail, wouldn't have it any other way, and being I'm a by-the-book lawman myself— and the most decorated deputy in Marshal Vail's stable—I wouldn't, either."

2

Behunek cast the young lawman a dubious look. "Most decorated badge-toter in Vail's stable, you say?"

"That's right."

"What about that one they call Longarm?" said Baron, staring skeptically at the young man over the rim of his speckled blue cup. "I thought he was the most decorated."

"Nah, he's just the biggest braggart," scoffed Parsons, giving his six-shooter another twirl, then dropping it smoothly into the hand-tooled holster on his right hip. "Old and washed up, if you ask me. Like an old dog. More interested in gettin' his ashes hauled than fightin' criminals anymore. That's why Marshal Vail sent me up here, 'stead of him."

"Sounds like you don't got much respect for ole Longarm," observed Miller, leaning back against a log, his Spencer carbine across his thighs. "But you sure dress like him. You got the Prince Albert coat and the tobacco-colored hat. Even wear the same kind of mustache, though yours ain't quite as full as ole Longarm's."

The others chuckled. Parsons's pale cheeks colored as he pinched his mustache repeatedly between his thumb and index finger. "How the hell would *you* know if his mustache is any *fuller* than mine?"

"He come through Diamondback a few months ago, lookin' for mail robbers," said Miller, grinning at the deputy's obvious indignation.

"Why, lookee there," Behunek said, staring at the young lawman's feet. "I never noticed it before, but he's even wearin' low-heeled cavalry boots—just like I seen ole Longarm wear!"

The others laughed mockingly, throwing their heads back on their shoulders, their guffaws drowning out the murmur of the river south of their coffee fire, beyond a small aspen copse where their horses foraged.

Parsons glared at each man in turn, his slender jaw set, face nearly the same rust red as his hair and mustache.

Slowly, fuming, he gained his feet and set his hands on the pearl grips of his twin .45s.

"I believe we've taken a long enough break, gentleman," he intoned, nostrils flaring, enunciating each word clearly. "If you think you can haul your lazy asses up, we'd best get moving. I'd like to reach the site of the mountain man's last killing before sundown."

"Hey, look at that," chuckled Behunek. "He's a good three, four inches shorter than ole Longarm, too!"

As the others roared, Parsons turned and began striding swiftly toward the horses. He was only ten yards away when he stopped suddenly, wheeled back toward the group still seated around the fire, and clawed his right pistol from his hip.

Crouching, he held the pistol just above the tied-down holster, the barrel aimed at the group.

"Tarnation!" Miller cried, dropping his coffee cup.

The exclamation hadn't died on Miller's lips before Parson's pistol barked, spouting smoke and fire, the .45 slug ripping Miller's floppy-brimmed black hat from his head.

As the hat flew up and back, Parsons's pistol spoke twice more in quick succession, tearing off Behunek's plain cream Stetson and then Baron's ancient, leather-billed Union forage cap. The hats settled in the brush a good ten yards behind the men, like oversized autumn leaves, one after another, a round, ragged hole adorning each.

The three townsmen stared agape at Parsons, who gave a self-satisfied grin through the wafting powder smoke. He twirled the .45 and dropped it in his holster.

"Could Longarm do *that*?"

Parsons snorted, wheeled, and continued walking toward the horses.

Behind him, the three bareheaded townsmen shared wary glances.

• • •

An hour later, the four-man posse rounded a snag of boulders strewn about the base of the canyon wall to their right. As they were about to enter a broad meadow stretching between the rocky ridge and the Diamondback River, Deputy Johnny Parsons jerked back on the reins of the long-legged zebra dun he'd acquired from Miller's livery barn in town.

The three other men, each sporting a hole in his hat, stopped their own horses behind Parsons.

"What's the matter?" asked Miller, still sounding petulant after the hat shooting.

Staring straight ahead through the sunlit meadow of breeze-ruffled wheatgrass, Parsons held up his black-gloved right hand for silence. After a moment, the breeze picked up, rustling the grass and the leaves of the cottonwoods along the river, bringing a sound across the meadow.

At first, Parsons thought it was the faint tinkling of wind chimes. Then, gradually, as the breeze pushed against the young lawman's face, whipping his string tie over his shoulder, each note acquired a human aspect, and he realized it was the sound, muffled by distance and gently obscured by the breeze, of girls laughing and giggling.

They seemed to be down by the river.

"Shit," said Jan Behunek, sitting his mare off Parsons's dun's right hip. "It's those fucking Magnusson bitches!"

Parsons turned toward him, cocking a brick red brow.

Mike Baron said, his voice pitched with fear, "Just before he died, that soldier talked of being lured to the river by the sounds of girls' laughter."

"Just a coincidence," said Ned Miller, chewing the dead quirley in his teeth and staring through the trees along the sun-glistening Diamondback. "Ain't no way Magnusson and his daughters would still be around here, this close to town. Why, they killed those soldiers only another mile or so upstream!"

The sounds had faded for a moment. Now, as the wind

stirred the grass and leaves once more, they rose again, sounding for all the world like two young girls frolicking along the river . . .

"Most likely a prospecting family hereabouts," said Parsons to no one in particular. As he shucked the Winchester from his saddleboot, laying the rifle's barrel across his pommel, he added, "But we'd best check it out."

As he reined the zebra dun off the left side of the trail, he glanced behind at the others. "You men wait here. If I need you, I'll fire a shot."

"Fine by me, Mr. Lawman, sir," growled Baron, holding the reins of his shying horse taut against his chest.

Parsons booted the dun toward the river. Three-quarters of the way to the trees along the bank, he checked the horse down, leaped nimbly from the saddle, dropped the reins, and continued into the trees on foot, holding his rifle high across his chest.

He squatted behind an aspen bole and looked out over the river. The sound of laughter was crisp and clear in the high, dry mountain air. Girls, all right. Two or three having a good old time a little ways downstream. Parsons could make out two heads bobbing in a sunny patch about fifty yards away.

Behind Parsons, his horse whinnied. The lawman turned to see the horse shying and pulling back against its ground-tied reins.

Ignoring the jittery horse, Parsons followed the sounds through the trees and crouched once more behind a tree bole atop the shallow cutbank. As he cast his gaze into the river, he froze, one eye narrowing and twitching slightly at the corner.

Out in the middle of the shallow stream, two girls—one with long, coal black hair, the other a golden blonde—frolicked around a four-foot waterfall. Neither wore a stitch, and their smooth skin, one Indian dark, the other Viking-pale, glistened in the waterfall's tumbling spray.

They crawled among the rocks, the water foaming around them. Wrestling like river sprites, they tugged at each other's arms or feet, plucking at toes and nipples, their full, round breasts bouncing against their chests, their plump asses turning this way and that, like ripe cantaloupes jostling in a wheelbarrow, reflecting the westering sun.

At once chilly with apprehension and warmed by desire, Parsons crouched, frozen, riveted.

The Indian-dark girl climbed to the top of the falls and sat down, dangling her long, brown legs over the foaming cascade. The blonde climbed up to where the dark one sat and, laughing, crawled up between the dark girl's legs and spread the other's knees with her hands.

The dark girl squealed and shook her long, soaked hair back from her face. She wrapped her arms around the blond girl's waist as the blonde leaned toward her, and they kissed hungrily, the blonde fondling the dark girl's big, swaying breasts.

The blonde rose higher, and the dark girl closed her mouth over the blonde's left, pink nipple, and together they fell back in the river, coupling amid the rocks and sliding water like lovers who hadn't seen each other in ages.

"*Tarnation!*"

Parsons snapped around, heart pounding, lowering his rifle barrel. Mike Baron stood before him, crouching to see over his shoulder. Miller stood to Baron's left, Behunek to his right. They all held rifles as they stared, transfixed, through the breeze-swept brush and bobbing branches.

"That's them," Baron exclaimed under his breath and pointing his rifle barrel at the river. "It's gotta be them." The old Spencer shook in his hands.

"I told you three to stay on the trail," Parsons said.

Ignoring the young lawman, Behunek hunkered down behind another tree and poked his bullet-torn hat back on his blond head as he stared at the giggling, chattering girls. "Now, wait a minute. I ain't exactly sure . . ."

Miller crouched behind Behunek. He, too, cast his gaze at the river, lower jaw falling slack. After a time, he ran the back of his hand across his mouth. "Christ, those girls are doin' downright . . . dirty things to one another . . . but there."

"That . . . that ain't natural," said Baron, who crept forward to hunker down in the brush before Parsons.

"I told you men to stay on the trail!" Parsons repeated, keeping his voice down. "If those are the two girls we're looking for, Magnusson himself is likely hereabouts."

The young lawman turned his head slowly, sweeping the trees to both sides, then the meadow behind him and the trail beyond, where the townsmen's three horses lowered their heads to forage the needle grass.

A chill ran up the young lawman's spine. "The old bastard could have a bead on us right now."

"That old killer ain't necessarily nowhere near here," said Miller in a faraway voice as he stared at the two girls frolicking atop the waterfall. "We can't be sure these two are his daughters. They could be Mel Ramie's girls. He's got him one towhead and one half-breed, too. We're too far away. I can't see 'em clear enough to be sure."

Parsons turned to the tall liveryman and was instantly distracted by the black-haired girl suddenly throwing the blonde onto her back. The blonde screamed. Laughing, the black-haired girl crawled on top of her and, placing both hands on the blonde's round breasts, began running her tongue down the blonde's belly toward her crotch.

The blonde shook her head from side to side and raised her knees. Her groans rose above the river's gurgle.

Parsons felt his face and loins warm. He didn't like what these girls were doing to him, how they'd captured not only his attention but his imagination, made him not want to think of anything else. As the dark-haired girl dropped her head down even lower on the blonde's belly, Parson raked his eyes toward Miller.

"How many prospectors' daughters cavort like *that* around *here*?" he scoffed, his voice thick in his throat. He jerked his head around, wary of an ambush. "You men stay here and keep an eye out for the old mountain man. I'm gonna head upstream, cross the river, and investigate the other shore."

When none of them said anything, Parsons turned to them. "Look alive, goddamnit!"

"You got it, Marshal," said Baron, not turning his head from the river.

"Whatever you do," Parsons said, "don't leave these trees. And for chrissakes, don't go into the river!"

Miller turned to him, beetling his gray brows. "We're not tinhorns, marshal. We'll keep a sharp eye out for Magnusson. We'll be coverin' ya. Don't you worry."

Parsons looked at the three men crouched in the brush, all three staring, mesmerized, toward the river. The young lawman shook his head and cursed as he turned and began walking upstream. When he was fifty yards beyond the waterfall, he looked around. Judging that he was alone at this section of the river, he stepped out from the bank and hopscotched rocks to the other side, once slipping and filling his right boot with water.

On the opposite bank, he took a slow look around, then sat down, set his rifle beside him, pulled off his boot, and poured out the water. When he'd tugged the boot back on, he rose, grabbed his rifle, and followed the girls' caroming laughter downstream while inspecting every boulder and brush snag for their kill-happy father, Magnus Magnusson.

Thirty yards from where the girls were entangled atop the waterfall—engaged in some sort of wrestling hold, it appeared, one yowling with mock pain—Parsons stopped. From a rocky hollow to his left, where the ground rose gently toward the southern canyon wall, smoke curled skyward.

Parsons adjusted his grip on his Winchester and headed toward the concealed fire, setting each boot down carefully, wincing as the soaked one chirped softly, like a baby bird. He looked back toward the river.

The girls were both sitting up Indian style, facing each other and playing patty-cake, breasts jiggling each time they slapped their hands together. Parsons looked beyond them, at the other side of the stream. No sign of the three townsmen crouched in the weeds.

The young lawman was half-surprised they hadn't descended on the two girls by now, throwing themselves on the pair like wild pack dogs on a crippled fawn.

He stopped four feet from the snag and leaned left, casting his gaze into the hollow. He could see only the tops of two dancing flames. Swallowing, ignoring his pounding heart, he took one step left, then bolted forward, leaping an ancient deadfall and extending the Winchester straight out from his left hip.

"Hold it, Mag—"

He stopped. The hollow was vacant. Only the fire with a coffeepot sitting a few inches from the glowing coals. Three coffee cups were lined up along the far side of the fire ring. A couple of saddles and bridles were piled beneath a cedar, and while Parsons couldn't see them, he heard the crunch of horses chewing grass, probably in the heavier brush at the base of the canyon wall.

The hair at the back of his neck pricked as he moved around the fire, peering into the middle distance.

Behind him, a rifle cracked. Parsons leaped a good foot in the air. His right boot landed awkwardly atop a deadfall, and he fell, dropping his rifle.

On the other side of the river, where he'd left Baron and Behunek, a man screamed.

Parsons extricated his right boot from the deadfall's branches, scrambled onto his hands and knees, grabbed his rifle, and heaved himself to his feet.

Another rifle crack, another scream, then another shot.

Parsons ran back toward the river, leaping rocks and tufts of bunchgrass. He stopped just before he hit the stream. Mike Baron leaped off the opposite bank and into the river, screaming and clutching his right shoulder as he ran, splashing, toward Parsons.

"It's him!" Baron screamed. "Good God, it's hi—"

The grocer's voice was clipped short by the roar of a rifle. As smoke puffed in the foliage behind Baron, the man's chest opened up, spouting blood. The man's head snapped back as the bullet thrust him forward. He hit the water face-first, arms and legs spread wide as he lolled in the current, dead.

The grocer's splash hadn't settled before Parsons dropped to one knee, snapped the Winchester to his shoulder, aimed at the billowing smoke, and fired three quick shots into the shrubs on the other side of the river. He ejected the spent shell, which clattered on the rocks behind him. As he rammed a fresh cartridge into the rifle's breech, he waded into the river, holding the rifle taut against his shoulder, staring down the barrel at the opposite shore.

He was halfway across the stream, heart sounding like a tom-tom in his ears, before he remembered the girls. He glanced to his left. His breath caught in his throat and his heart did a somersault.

Both girls were crouched behind a thumb of rocks sticking up from the edge of the waterfall. Both had carbines in their hands, and they were aiming the rifles at Parsons. They no longer looked quite as much like girls—at least, not in the face. Their eyes owned a feral, savage cast, and their lips were turned down grimly. They looked like animals. The wet hair hanging straight down both sides of their faces slid around in the breeze.

"No!" Parsons cried involuntarily, swinging his own rifle toward them.

He'd swung the gun only six inches before the girls triggered their carbines at the same time. The twin smoke

11

puffs tore and dispersed as both bullets took Parsons high on his chest. He twisted around and stumbled sideways, triggering his own Winchester into the river then dropping the gun as he hit the water and lay on his back, the bullets searing him like war lances.

"Oh . . . oh, Jesus . . . !"

Staring straight up at the sky, he felt his blood welling out of him. Christ, he thought, that was a dunderheaded move. Longarm never would have forgotten about the two girls . . .

As if his own thoughts had summoned them, the blonde and the brunette appeared in his field of vision, staring down at him. They held their rifles low across their thighs.

The breeze had dried their naked bodies, which were just as incredible as they'd appeared before—the round-hipped, firm-thighed, full-breasted epitomes of perfect female flesh. It was their eyes that turned Parsons's stomach, drew his balls up into his belly. They were savage, unfeeling, malicious in the most coldly objective way imaginable.

As if from somewhere far away, Parsons heard someone striding toward him through the water. As a bearded, hatted head came into view, a wet muzzle prodded his right cheek. He smelled the dog before he saw it, and jerked away.

No, not a dog. Not many dogs that size. The animal facing him—mottled brown and gunmetal gray, with a long, thick snoot and eyes even more feral than those of the women and the bearded man staring down at him—was a wolf. Big and lean, it drew its furry lips back from teeth white as porcelain and sharp as a Bowie knife.

The bearded man had to be nearly seven feet tall, his face nearly entirely covered by the thick, curly, cinnamon beard which was lanced with white, as though from a scar on the left cheek. He prodded the wolf away with his rifle barrel.

"Get away, Moon," the man growled, his voice deep and resonant.

"Lookee that, Pa," said the blonde, still staring down at Parsons, prodding his badge with her rifle. "He's law."

"Sure 'nough," the bearded man grumbled. He dipped his chin to his chest, staring straight down at Parsons. "You after me, lawdog?"

Parsons's lights were dimming fast. He just stared up at the three savage faces staring down at him, feeling the wolf sniffing at his forehead. He kept thinking, Why didn't I remember the girls? Longarm wouldn't have forgotten the girls.

"Well, that's just too damn bad for you!" The mountain man grinned.

The last thing Parsons saw was the rifle's bore closing down over his right eye. He didn't even hear the shot that killed him.

Chapter 2

Deputy United States Marshal Custis Long, known by friend and foe as Longarm, opened his eyes, pulled the silk sheets and heavy wool comforter down from his face, and stared into the spacious room before him, a subtle but provocative women's perfume touching his nostrils.

Only a misty, opal light washed through the window to his right, so he could barely make out the big armoire and heavy, ebony dresser beyond the end of the vast bed he was lying in.

Between the two obviously valuable pieces of furniture hung a gilt-framed painting nearly as large as one entire wall in his own rented digs on the poor side of Cherry Creek. Before the painting, a chair faced him. It, too, looked expensive, but Longarm couldn't even begin to describe from what rare materials it had been so carefully, gracefully constructed.

The chair didn't interest the lawman all that much, anyway. What caught the brunt of his attention was the black fishnet stocking hanging from one corner of the dresser by an even frillier red garter belt. Not far from the dangling toe of the stocking, a dainty high-heeled, patent-leather shoe lay on its side, as if casually tossed there.

14

Nearer the bed lay several pieces of Longarm's own clothes—white cotton shirt, fawn vest, and one low-heeled cavalry boot. The boot was partially concealed by a pair of women's silk panties so sheer that they appeared little more than a smudge on Longarm's worn boot. They were so thin and insubstantial, Longarm decided as he lay half-dozing and half-savoring the luxuriant surroundings, that he could no doubt stuff the entire garment under one cheek.

He looked around the rest of the well-appointed room, spying more of his own clothes and those of his companion strewn about the ornate furniture and deep-carpeted floor—his string tie was hanging off a gilt wall taper—and remembered the theater last night and the lovely, raven-haired queen he'd attended it with—Cynthia Larimer, niece of General William H. Larimer himself, Denver's founding father.

Cynthia, a debutante who'd attended one of the grandest finishing schools on the East Coast and who spent as much time traipsing around foreign continents as this one, was visiting Denver more and more often of late, ever since she and Longarm had been introduced at the last governor's ball. Mostly, she arranged her visits to coincide with the absence of her uncle and aunt.

That made it easier for her and Longarm, after a late night on Larimer Street attending balls, the opera, the theater, or somesuch other foolishness she dragged him to as a prequisite for getting into her bloomers, to frolick away the early morning hours playing hide-and-seek, naked, in the Larimers' grand hallways and smoking parlors and libraries.

Last night's activity had begun on the front porch before Cynthia had even gotten the key in the lock. It had continued to the foyer for about eight more minutes, then to the large wooden food preparation table in the vast, stone-floored kitchen for nine or ten more.

From there, the fervor abating enough that they could more fully appreciate the journey as well as the destination, they'd moved to an ottoman in the cigar parlor, to a fainting couch in the second-floor hall under the stairs, then, finally, at around two in the morning, to the very bed upon which Longarm now lay.

The memories of last night were so vivid—he could even hear the girl's passionate groans echoing off the cavernous ceiling as he'd plundered her in the kitchen—that Longarm's loins stirred.

He turned to the brass-and-cherrywood clock on the bedside table. Not even six yet. He turned full around to face the other side of the bed, and frowned. The covers were pulled back. A dent remained in the cream silk pillow where Cynthia's lovely head had reclined, and the silk sheets still bore the slender form of her body.

The girl herself, however, was nowhere to be seen.

He'd no sooner registered her absence than he heard something. He lifted his head from the pillow, rising onto his elbows.

Soft footsteps sounded, the light slap of bare feet on wooden stairs. They were accompanied by the rattling of fine china. As the padding of bare feet on the hall carpet runner grew louder, as well as the dainty rattles of fine china on tin, the perfume fragrance intensified.

The door latch clicked, the long brass handle dropped, and the door swung open.

"Cust-isss?"

The girl's slender silhouette entered the room, her long, raven hair falling from beneath a man's flat-brimmed hat, a long, unlit cigar slanting from her mouth. She held a silver serving tray before her. As she stood beside the bed, Longarm stared up at her, his heart twisting with desire.

The girl—he figured she was in her early twenties though she'd never told him her exact age—wore Longarm's own threadbare long underwear. They'd been washed so many times that they barely fit Longarm's tall, muscular frame anymore. He owned better pairs, but they'd been in his landlady's washtub when he'd dressed for last evening.

16

On the slight girl before him this shrunken pair sagged like a pink army tent, the unbuttoned, V-necked top falling down to reveal a delectable portion of her full, round, creamy breasts, the nipples prodding the thin cotton like derringer bores. As overlarge as the garment was in the shoulders and chest, it clung alluringly to the full, tapering roundness of Cynthia's hips and taut thighs.

The hat on her head was his own snuff brown Stetson, and the cigar between her teeth was one of his three-for-a-nickel cheroots he must have left downstairs in his Prince Albert coat pocket.

Cynthia grinned. "Hi, there."

"Mornin'." His voice was thick, his eyes tracing the row of bone buttons on his underwear top as they angled down her right breast and over the nipple peeking at him like a mouse from its hole.

"I'm wearing your underwear. Hope you don't mind. I was chilly."

"I won't arrest you if you get out of them pronto."

"Custis, now, haven't you had enough of that? I myself feel like a mare that's been rode hard by a whole herd and put up wet." Cynthia giggled. "Look." She set the tray on his lap and sat down on the bed, leaning across his knees. "I brought you breakfast."

Longarm had been so entranced by the girl's figure in his own underwear that he hadn't noticed the bottle of Maryland rye atop the tray, flanking the two bone-china cups, steaming silver server, and a plate filled with grapes and orange wedges, another with buttered toast.

Balancing the tray on his knees, he slid up against the headboard and reached for the bottle. "So you did! Thank you mighty kindly." He plucked the bottle off the tray, popped the cork, and threw back a liberal shot. "Where are my manners?" he said lowering the bottle, running a hand across his mustache, and extending the rye to the girl. "A wake-me-up?"

17

Cynthia laughed, accepted the bottle, and tipped it back. Her eyes popped wide and she made several unladylike gagging sounds as the liquid hit her throat. Lowering the bottle, she pressed the back of her wrist to her mouth, swallowing hard.

"How can you stand that stuff?" she croaked.

"That's nectar of the gods, girl!"

"Enough!" She swallowed hard, eyes bulging. "Time for something a little more civilized for us both." She gave him back the bottle and poured coffee into each cup.

When Longarm had added another shot of the rye to his java, he corked the bottle, set it on the floor, then sat back as, coffee in one hand, fruit plate in the other, Cynthia scooted up beside him and began feeding them both with her hands.

It was one of her morning rituals. Longarm didn't mind. The problem was that by the time she'd slowly slipped a couple of grapes and orange slices into his mouth, sometimes even using her own mouth to do so, he was so damn horny that his head swam giddily in spite of his throbbing hangover from the night before.

Now she pulled away from him after stuffing an orange wedge into his mouth with her tongue and, grinning, chewed what remained of the wedge, the juice running down her full, red lips to her chin and down her long, creamy neck. Her eyes danced in the dawn light penetrating the curtained window behind Longarm.

He looked at her breasts, both revealed by his billowing underwear top, nipples jutting like pink rubber knobs.

"Now, Custis, don't get in a hurry," Cynthia admonished huskily. "We need our nourishment."

A bead of orange juice ran into the deep V between her breasts. Longarm leaned down and licked the bead from her smooth, warm skin. She gave a shiver and chuckled.

"Ooo!"

Longarm smacked his lips as he sat up, lifted the silver

tray from his lap, and dropped his legs to the floor.

"Custis, we're not finished yet," Cynthia said primly. "We each still have two oranges and two grapes left."

"I've had enough," Longarm said as he padded naked across the room and set the tray on the dresser. "Of that."

He turned and strode back to the bed. Sitting up beside his pillow, her long legs doubled beneath her, breasts hanging out of the underwear top, Cynthia stared at him. She still wore his hat. She slipped another grape between her lips and opened her mouth to speak but stopped when her eyes dropped to his jutting shaft.

"Oh, my," she breathed, slowly chewing the grape.

Longarm held out his hand. "Not that I'll be needin' it for a bit, but I'll be takin' back my underwear, young lady."

Eyes riveted to Longarm's swollen cock, Cynthia swallowed, wiggled her shoulders until the garment had fallen to her waist, then crawled to the edge of the bed before his jutting shaft. She wriggled like a snake until the washworn underwear had slipped over her hips and down her thighs to bunch up around her ankles.

She kicked them off the other side of the bed, rose onto her elbows, and ran her cheek along the side of Longarm's shaft. She pulled her head back and wrapped a hand around the throbbing member, staring at it as a sultry smile touched her lips.

Longarm sighed, blood surging, and plucked his hat from her head, tossed it away.

Cynthia stuck her tongue out, touched it to the bulging end of Longarm's dong. He dug his toes into the carpet, almost unloading right there. He managed to hold back while silently humming the first few bars of an old hymn he'd learned as a child.

"On a hill far away stood an old rugged cross,
The emblem of suffering and shame . . ."

Looking down, he watched her, groaning softly, slide her mouth down over his organ and move her head toward his groin, the heat of her tickling tongue setting him on fire.

"So I'll cherish the old rugged cross
Till my trophies at last I lay down . . ."

When she'd taken as much as she could, making a slight gagging sound, she pulled back slowly until her lips swelled over the head of his organ and popped off. Spittle stringing between her lips and his cock, she glanced up at him coyly.

"Sure you wouldn't like another orange?"

"Certain sure," he grated out, guiding her head back onto his cock then grinding his feet into the carpet as she began throwing the blocks to him, making loud sucking and choking noises as she worked.

The blood surged with more vigor through his veins, and he threw his head back on his shoulders and stretched his lips back from his teeth.

Unable to hold back any longer, he spread his feet and let himself go, his hands clutching her shoulders as, knees bent slightly and leaning back from his waist, he jettisoned his seed down the frantically opening and closing throat of General Larimer's bewitching niece.

Forty-five minutes later, having taken a whore's bath and dressed while Cynthia, spent from the blow job and one more hard, parting romp, dozed beneath the sheets, Longarm let himself out the back door of the Larimer mansion and lit a three-for-a-nickel cheroot in the lee of the brick carriage house.

The last time he'd left the Larimer place, after a night and morning similar to the one he'd just enjoyed, someone had tried to bore a bullet through his forehead. The shooter had been a relative of an outlaw he'd kicked out with a shovel after said outlaw had ambushed him from the privy behind Longarm's own rented digs on the other side of Cherry Creek. The relative was old history now, too, but that didn't mean there weren't more relatives of other dead or incarcerated men on his trail.

It was a cautious Longarm, puffing his cigar and keeping his .44 loose in the cross-draw holster on his left hip, who made his way down Sherman Avenue to the heart of the waking city, hearing the meadowlarks pipe, the blackbirds caw, and the coal wagons squawk and rattle over the cobbles.

The smell of wood and coal smoke tinged the damp breeze blowing in from the prairie. As he made his way to a bathhouse not far from the Federal Building, the sun rose from the prairie to set fire to the snow-tipped peak of Mount Evans rising above of the Front Range in the west.

After a bath and a shave, and pleased as punch no one had tried to clean his clock this morning—having to parry lead after lovemaking was no way to start a day—he strode up the broad stone steps of the Federal Building. He wove his way among the pretty young office clerks in their summer-weight frocks and shining hair, and climbed to the building's second floor.

"Mornin', Henry!" Longarm stepped through the oak door on which the words "U.S. MARSHAL WILLIAM VAIL" were stenciled in gold-leaf lettering, and tossed his hat on the rack.

The pimple-faced clerk pounding a sandwich of onion skins and carbon paper with his typewriter keys kept his nearsighted eyes on the newfangled machine and continued pecking away with the practiced ease of a true paper pusher.

"Go right in. Marshal Vail has been waiting for you, Deputy Long."

Longarm paused before the secretary's tidy desk. He was about to mention that he was exactly two minutes early—some time ago he'd turned over a new leaf of punctuality—but what was the point? Reputations were as hard to reconfigure as the planets and stars.

He merely chuckled, knocked once on Billy's door, and went in. "Mornin', Chief!"

"Jesus Christ, you're early!" The pudgy, balding man behind the desk, swathed in cigar smoke, turned to the banjo clock on the wall to his left. "A full two minutes!"

"Billy, you noticed!"

"Are you all right?" With the stubby cigar in his right hand Vail gestured at the red Moroccan leather chair. "You better have a seat." He beetled his sandy brows, inspecting Longarm ironically. "But, hell, you look all right. Don't appear fever-flushed. In fact, I swear, Custis, you're looking even lighter on your feet than usual. And your eyes are dancing like those of a carnival barker who's just spied a whole gaggle of wealthy tinhorns!"

Longarm angled the chair before the chief marshal's desk and sat down. "They are?"

Vail sat back in his own swivel chair, voice booming around the sparsely furnished office. "Don't tell me you're fucking General Larimer's niece again!"

"I don't much like to call it fucking," Longarm said, grinning. "Much too crass. I prefer lovemaking, Chief."

"It's fucking, and you know it. You two have been goin' at it like a couple of back-alley dogs. What—the general's out of town again, so you two have that big old house to your nymphomaniac selves?"

Longarm opened his mouth to object, but Vail cut him off. He poked the cigar at Longarm for emphasis. "If the general ever finds out you and that niece he prizes almost as much as his Thoroughbred racing horses are using his house for a stud barn, he's liable to come in here with a double-barreled shotgun. I just hope for my sake and Henry's that the old bastard can aim straight."

"Don't worry, Chief. I don't think the general's weak heart would make it up the Federal Building steps."

"No, he'll probably wait and ambush you from his carriage house some early morning while you're walking out his back door buttoning your fly."

"He might as well join the club."

"Anyway, enough chatter about your infamous sex life. We got trouble."

Longarm set his right cavalry boot on his left knee and flicked coal ash from his trousers. "Trouble's our bread and butter, Chief."

"You remember Deputy Parsons?"

"Deputy Johnny Parsons. Of course. You've made me work with the little privy rat a time or two, and I do believe I told you he'd been promoted way before his time. Say, about *twenty years* before his time. Why, that younker can't even . . ."

"He's dead," Vail said, sitting back in his chair.

Longarm stared at his boss, chagrined.

"Killed up north last week," Billy said. "I just got word yesterday. His body's coming in today on the flier."

"Can't say as I'm surprised. That kid was a corpse waiting to get cold. Who cooled him down, Chief?"

"Goddamndest thing I ever heard of," Vail said, wagging his head and taking a couple of big, shallow puffs off his cigar. "There's a crazy mountain man up in the bluffs and canyons west of Diamondback, just north of Fort Collins. Magnus Magnusson's the name. Lived with a couple squaws up near Ute Peak back in the old days, when there was still a market for beaver furs.

"Anyway, this Magnusson is crazier than a tree full of owls. He's got two daughters just as crazy and wild as he is. They're preying on the miners around the Diamondback River, up around the Neversummer Range and the Mummies. The girls sort of act like sirens, getting the prospectors' guard down with their feminine wiles—apparently they're both prettier'n a coupla speckled pups, with jugs the size of watermelons—and just when they're at their

23

most vulnerable, Magnusson comes in and shoots or stabs 'em. Him and the girls make off with the prospectors' pokes or any other valuables."

"How did Johnny Parsons end up toe-down, Chief? I wouldn't think old Magnusson and his daughters are even a federal problem. Sounds local."

"I'm getting to that." Vale took another puff from his cigar and waved the smoke away, squinting. "The trouble all started about six months ago. Finally, when seven or eight miners had been murdered, the sheriff, Merle Blassingame, wired me for help. He just didn't have the manpower to put a stop to it."

"So you sent Parsons."

"Yes, I sent Parsons, goddamnit!" Billy yelled, slamming his fist on his broad, mahogany desk, knocking the first couple inches of a two-foot stack of papers onto the floor. Ignoring the mess, he jerked his chair toward the window. "Didn't sound like a job for a real lawman. I figured, hell, how hard could it be for the kid to go up there and hire a guide to take him up that canyon and haul an old mountain man and his two daughters down to the local hoosegow?"

"Sounds easy enough, Boss, but you know Johnny."

"Yeah, I *knew* Johnny. Fancied himself Custis Long in his brown hat and cavalry boots. Shit, I think he smoked the same cigars as you."

"The kid was downright frightening. Whenever I seen him, I thought I was seein' myself in the mirror about fifteen years ago." Longarm shrugged. "Didn't care for me much, though."

"Shit, he idolized you. But he didn't *like* you because he knew you didn't respect him. It was his old man's political connections that got him the goddamn deputy's job in the first place. His only training was the Army. Well, now he's dead and his old man, Julian Parsons, is demanding justice."

24

"You want me to go up there and hunt down old Magnusson and his sirens, Chief?"

Vail was staring out the window, a pensive expression on his fleshy, clean-shaven face. His cigar smoldered in his right hand, that elbow propped on the edge of the desk.

Longarm felt sorry for his boss. He wouldn't have taken on the pressure of the chief marshal's job for all the money in the world. To think that a leaner, tougher Billy Vail had once been a Texas Ranger, a cap-and-ball blazing in each fist . . .

Suddenly, Billy swung toward Longarm, scowling, his chair squawking loudly. "Does a bear shit in the woods? Of course I want them brought in. And make it fast! I just got two cables—one from Parsons's old man and one from the governor, both urging me to spare no expense in avenging the kid's death."

Billy leaned forward to regard Longarm with vehemence. "Now, neither you nor I, Custis, give a diddly goddamn about that little make-believe badge-toter, but, political pressure or not, I *did hire him.* So my ass is over the fire here, you understand?"

"Personally, Chief, I'm more concerned about the prospectors those three are preying on than avenging that rich little privy snipe, but I get your drift." Longarm dropped his right foot to the floor and sat up in his chair. "Henry's working on my pay vouchers, I take it?"

Vail nodded. "He's got your train ticket, too. The flier leaves at noon. Rent a horse at Longmont, then head for Diamondback. Your contact there is Sheriff Blassingame. Merle Blassingame. I've never met him, but you'll know where to find him. He'll know someone who can guide you up the canyon. After killing Parsons, Magnusson and his two heifers are probably holing up pretty deep in the mountains. You'll need a good guide to root 'em out, most likely."

"Got it, Chief."

Longarm stood and headed for the door. He'd set his hand on the knob when Billy's voice turned him back around.

Vail was grinning but there wasn't an ounce of humor in it. "And, Custis . . . please remember that, while Magnusson's daughters are both right pretty and, I understand, built like a choirboy's wet dream, they're also deadly."

"Don't worry, Billy." Longarm grinned. "They won't be catching me with *my* pants down!"

With a parting salute and a wink, Longarm opened the door and went out.

Chapter 3

Longarm enjoyed a corned beaf sandwich and two beers at the Black Cat Saloon before heading to his rented flat to pick up his rifle, saddlebags, and McClelland saddle. He informed his persnickety landlady he'd be gone for a few days, then hitched a ride on a firewood dray angling toward the Union Depot in Denver's bustling heart.

The north-headed flier wasn't crowded, so Longarm managed a nap on the worn cowhide seat, compensating himself for his lack of rest and his overindulgence in both drink and Miss Larimer the night before. The train chugged through the blond-grass prairie in the shadow of the Rockies' magnificent Front Range, the wheels clacking somnolently beneath his head, the smell of steam and coal smoke in his nose.

When the train stopped halfway between Denver and Cheyenne, at the little mining and ranching berg of Longmont, over which Long's Peak towered like a giant, snow-tipped sentinel, it was a better-rested if still-groggy federal lawman who gathered his gear from the overhead rack and stepped down into the village's dusty, golden sunlight.

Longarm rented a fine, broad-chested sorrel gelding at the Federated Livery and Feed Barn and trimmed out the horse with his own McClelland, preferring the lightweight cavalry pad to the more cumbersome stock saddles found throughout the frontier. He snugged his Winchester into the boot, then secured his bedroll and saddlebags behind the low cantle.

With a wave to the beefy hostler eyeing him skeptically from the paddock, he left the sleepy town in its grove of cottonwoods and aspens, crossed the St. Vrain River, and jogged northwest through the clay-colored shelves and pine-studded rimrocks rolling up toward the grand, fir-studded peaks he could no longer see from this low angle.

He made Diamondback in the late afternoon.

The town was a forlorn little collection of sun-baked hovels strewn about the prairie where the Diamondback River curled out of its canyon to arc southward toward its confluence with Crow Creek and the South Platte River. The village was wedged between rimrocks and surrounded by prairie dog towns and cedar-studded knolls. Its main street, called Diamondback Avenue, was two blocks long, with about a hundred feet of open, sun-scorched broom grass, rabbit brush, and sage between its false-fronted business buildings—most constructed of brick or logs or both.

As Longarm rode through town, three pudgy boys in knickers were playing cowboys with stick rifles in the middle of the wide, rutted street, a black-and-white collie nipping at their heels and barking. Two bearded men in prospectors' garb stood before an overloaded mountain wagon, passing a bottle and conversing with a rangy bald man in a long, green apron and armbands. A two-story building with a long loading dock and announcing itself as the "Occidental Mercantile" heaved purple shade over the men and the wagon.

Longarm reined up at the edge of the shade, and the three men eyed him with guarded speculation. He rarely wore his badge anywhere but in his wallet, feeling it made too shiny a target for would-be bushwackers. "Can someone direct me to the marshal's office?"

The prospectors just stared at him, the one with a silver-streaked bib beard holding the uncorked brown bottle protectively against his frayed coveralls.

The bald man—the mercantile owner, no doubt—jerked a thumb behind him. "It's the stone shack tucked away in the rabbit brush back behind my store. You won't find the marshal there, however." He acquired a strangely sheepish expression and bowed his head at the Horsetooth Saloon west one block and on the other side of the street.

Longarm pinched his hat brim at the bald man, then neck-reined the sorrel toward the saloon—a broad log building with a brush awning over its wide front porch. The lawman drew the sorrel up to the hitchrack, left of the six other mounts standing before the stock tank, hang-headed and tail-swishing, and swung down from the saddle.

As he looped the reins over the rack, he glanced across the street. Three men in dusty trail garb sat on the board-walk before Alfonse's Tonsorial Parlor, their boots in the street, staring at Longarm from beneath the broad brims of their hats. The three wore pistols in tied-down holsters. One held a sawed-off shotgun across his thighs.

Longarm's instincts told him the men weren't merely waiting around for a friend to get a shave and a haircut. What they were doing, he had no idea, but he didn't like their looks. If he'd been the local law, he'd have encouraged them to mount up and spread their cheer elsewhere.

Since he wasn't the local law, he only eyed the three as he shucked his Winchester from his saddle boot, then laid the barrel across his shoulder as he stepped onto the saloon's porch and pushed through the batwings.

Standing just inside the door, he raked his eyes around the room, taking in the five men sitting negligently around two tables against the far right wall, and two more men occupying the shadows at the rear. Two of the men from the larger group were sipping from coffee mugs, while the others in the group had beer schooners or shot glasses before them.

The coffee drinkers were playing checkers. The three others appeared to be taking turns cutting a card deck Red Dog style. They all glanced at Longarm with passing interest before returning their attention to their games.

Longarm didn't see a marshal's star among them.

He sauntered up to the bar, where a tall, burly gent with short-cropped salt-and-pepper hair and frosty blue eyes was trimming his nails with a Bowie knife. He seemed reluctant to take his eyes off the two men sitting in the room's rear shadows.

"I'm lookin' for the marshal," Longarm said, setting his rifle on the bar top and casting another look over the batwings, at the three men before the tonsorial parlor. They were staring menacingly toward the saloon.

The blue-eyed barman glanced at him, mild annoyance in his gaze, then jerked his head to indicate the two at the rear.

"Sorta *occupied* at the moment," the man muttered.

Longarm peered into the shadows. The two men sat at a table between two square-hewn ceiling joists. On the papered wall behind them was a large painting of a naked brunette riding a tall, black horse in a lush tropical jungle, a lion eyeing her hungrily from the dense foliage.

The man facing Longarm, his back to the wall, had long, blond hair, a deerskin jacket over a cream shirt, and an olive green slouch hat. From this distance and because of the smoky shadows, Longarm couldn't tell much about his face, but he seemed medium-sized, possibly slightly delicate-featured.

A tin star peeked out from under his jacket flap.

The man who sat with his back to Longarm was short and stocky. He wore black slacks and a black vest over a red shirt. His black hat was on the table before him, and his longish, black hair was slicked straight back from his forehead. Wearing two pearl-gripped pistols in tied down holsters, he leaned forward across the table.

His head bobbed as he spoke in low but vehement tones. The blond-haired gent sat casually back in his own chair, a boot on a knee, head canted to one side, as if only vaguely interested in the black-haired gent's conversation.

"I'll take a rye while I wait," Longarm told the barman. "Got any Maryland?"

The big man frowned. "Any *what*?"

"Never mind." Longarm was glad he'd packed his own bottle in his saddlebags. You couldn't get much but coffin varnish out here in the tall and uncut. "Just give me a shot of whatever you got that won't blind me or take the thunder from my gun, if you get my drift."

Casting another glance toward the room's rear, the big man reached under the bar, automatically poured out a shot, and flicked the glass toward Longarm. The glass snugged against the Winchester's forestock. Longarm picked it up and sipped it.

It tasted like horse piss, chicken scratch, tin, and gunpowder. He'd tasted worse.

When he'd tossed a couple coins on the counter, he took another sip from the shot glass and peered again into the room's smoky back shadows. The marshal's jaws were moving, as if he was now doing the talking, though he was keeping his voice so low that Longarm couldn't make out a word.

Longarm turned away, then turned back quickly as the black-haired gent bounded straight back in his chair, both hands reaching for the pearl-butted pistols adorning his hand-tooled holsters.

He shouted, "Have it your way, you fuckin'—!"

The marshal bolted to his feet, blond hair bouncing on his shoulders as he lifted the table and shoved it into the black-haired man's chest. "*Ahh!*" the man raged, having raised his .45s only belly-high before the table slammed against him, sending him stumbling straight back.

A revolver popped twice, and Longarm saw two oval divots chew through the table's scarred, varnished surface. The black-haired gent lowered his head, throwing his shoulders forward and jerking, bellowing like a poleaxed mule as gunsmoke puffed up from the other side of the table.

Amid the sudden din, the blue-eyed barman ducked, yelling, "*Shit, I knew it!*"

Behind Longarm, someone shouted, "Fer chrissakes, *git* that badge-totin' ringtail!"

As the five gents sprang to their feet, clawing iron, Longarm slammed his shot glass down on the bar and reached for the Winchester. He rammed a shell into the breech. "Hold on—federal law!"

The words had about as much effect on the hard cases as spit would have on a prairie twister.

They were all shouting now, drawing iron, aiming at the back of the room, where the black-haired gent was flopping around on the floor like a landed fish and the marshal was giving the table a final toss to his left.

A bull-necked, red-haired gent seemed to have the drop on the local badge-toter. Longarm snapped his rifle to his shoulder, aimed, and fired.

The slug slammed into the big gent's left arm. He howled and fired his Schofield into the picture on the wall behind the marshal, who dropped to one knee and extended his own silver-plated Colt Navy.

The standing four hard cases all fired their revolvers at the same time, but Longarm's shout and shot had distracted them, and all shots peppered the wall behind the marshal, drilling more holes through the canvas and shattering a bracket lamp.

Longarm cocked and fired the Winchester. The hard case closest to him bellowed and spun, triggering a shot into the wagon-wheel chandelier over his head as he fell. The smell of kerosene mixed with powder smoke.

Meanwhile, the marshal took out one of the others, his shot punching the man through the long, vertical window in a shower of breaking glass.

Longarm flinched as a bullet curled the air over his left temple. He shuttled his gaze to the redhead he'd winged. The man was on his side near the player piano, raging above the angry, intermittent pistol pops and gritting his teeth as he thumbed back his revolver's hammer and aimed down the barrel at Longarm.

Longarm snapped the Winchester to his shoulder and drilled a neat, round hole through the man's freckled forehead, just above the bridge of his nose. The man lowered his gun, tripping the trigger, the slug slamming into the ass of a man the marshal had shot, evoking a scream the likes of which Longarm hadn't heard outside a pig lot on butchering day.

Longarm ejected the smoking spent shell, seated a fresh cartridge, dropped to a knee, and jerked his gaze right and left and back again.

All the hard cases were down, blood pooling, smoke wafting, howls rising to the rafters.

To his left, the marshal shouted, "*Falcon!*"

Longarm turned to see the black-haired gent hobbling up the wooden stairs at the back of the room, heels pounding the wood, spurs chinging.

The marshal aimed his Colt Navy at the stairs, tracking the fleeing black-clad gent. "Stop, goddamnit!"

Falcon disappeared over the top landing.

The marshal cursed again and ran to the stairs. As his long legs took the steps two at a time, his deerskin jacket winging open, Longarm saw shadows moving beyond the two front windows. He ran to the door and pushed through the batwings.

Stopping just outside the doors, he spread his feet and aimed the Winchester straight out from his hip.

The three who'd been sitting in front of the tonsorial parlor were walking toward the saloon, two holding pistols, the third—a curly-haired hombre in a checked shirt and rabbit-fur vest—holding the sawed-off shotgun straight out from his belly in both hands.

The three stopped suddenly, gazes locking on Longarm.

"You three are headed in the wrong direction," the lawman warned mildly. "A long, healthy life is either that way or that way." Keeping his eyes locked on the three hard cases, he jerked his head first to the left, then to the right.

He curled his upper lip and squeezed the rifle in his hands. The curly-haired hombre began edging his shotgun's barrel toward Longarm. "Who the fuck're you?"

"Custis Long, Deputy United States Marshal. And if the maw of that gut-shredder keeps inching my way, I'm the last son of a bitch you'll ever meet."

The man held the shotgun still. He glanced at the men on either side of him, then stared hard at Longarm.

Finally, he spat to one side and stretched his lips back from his teeth. "Shee-it."

He glanced at the man to his right and jerked his head to indicate the horses tied before the tonsorial parlor, from the front door of which poked the head of a bespectacled, mustachioed gent with pomaded hair and a wary look in his eyes.

The curly-haired gent rested the barrel of his gut-shredder over one shoulder and turned. The two others both followed suit—a Mexican and a bull-legged stringbean—heading back toward the horses.

The curly-haired gent hadn't taken two steps before he swung back around, dropping the shotgun's barrel to his left hand, and aiming it straight out from his belly at Longarm, a devilish smile slashing his face and making his gray eyes glitter.

Longarm, who'd kept the Winchester aimed at him, squeezed the trigger. He'd aimed at the center of the man's chest, but the man dodged right just enough to send the slug ripping across the top of his right shoulder, puffing dust from his shirt.

Longarm stepped forward, quickly levering a fresh shell and dropping to his knees as the Mexican triggered his Colt. The slug barked into the hitchrack near Longarm at the same time he drilled a .44 slug through the Mexican's right arm.

The bullet spun the man around to face the curly-headed gent. The curly-headed gent had dropped to one knee, cursing, face bunched with fury. Involuntarily, he squeezed both his shotgun's triggers.

Ka-boooom!

Both barrels of double-ought buck carved a pumpkin-sized hole through the Mexican's middle, lifting him two feet off the ground and throwing him straight back toward the saloon. His gut spewed viscera as he landed crossways atop a stock trough, screaming and thrashing like a tick impaled on the end of a pin.

As Longarm ejected the smoking shell casing, he snapped the Winchester to his shoulder, aiming quickly at the stringbean. The man had fired one round into the saloon's batwings behind Longarm and was thumbing back his Remington's hammer for another shot.

Longarm drilled one bullet through the slack of the man's vest as the man wheeled back and sideways, triggering a slug into the window behind Longarm, then running toward a stock trough on the other side of the street.

Longarm dropped to one knee, tracked the man with his Winchester, and fired. The stringbean screamed and reached for his right calf as he dove behind the trough. Spewing epithets salty enough to make the devil blush, he lifted his head, snaking his Remington over the stock trough's lip.

He hadn't gotten the barrel leveled before Longarm squeezed the Winchester's trigger once more.

The man jerked as the .44 round plunked into his forehead. Blood and brains painted the porch post behind him as he fell backward, losing his flat-brimmed hat and sagging against the steps climbing toward a women's clothing shop. His chin dropped, and his body jerked as though he'd been struck by lightning.

From the saloon's second story, boots pounded. There was the thud and crash of furniture and glass. A man shouted, "Merl, goddamnit!"

As Longarm raked his eyes from the smoky street and the three dead men, a body burst through a second-story window. Glass screamed as it rained toward the street, sheathing the black-clad gent called Falcon, who hit the ground boots first and rolled onto his belly as more glass rained down atop and around him.

His back rose and fell sharply.

Above him, the marshal poked his head through the broken window. The lawman angled his silver-plated Colt toward the street and fired, the report echoing off the store facades and jerking several shopkeepers back inside their front doorways.

The bullet spanged off a rock just left of Falcon, who jerked his head up and shook it, as if to clear the cobwebs.

When Falcon just lay there, propped on his arms, breathing hard and grunting, the marshal triggered another shot into the dirt to his right. The bullet sent up a little dust puff. Smoke wafted from the broken second-floor window.

Falcon cursed, rose first to his knees, then to his feet, and lumbered off toward the two horses remaining at the saloon's hitchrack, the others having ripped their reins free and galloped out of town during Longarm's dustup. Falcon walked, his torso twisted to one side, his left hand clutching his bloody right shoulder.

His face looked like raw burger. Broken shards dropped from his torn clothes like sleet from a late-autumn storm.

The very picture of misery, he ripped a claybank's reins from the hitchrack. Grunting, sighing, and cursing through gritted teeth, he took a good fifteen seconds getting his left boot into the stirrup, then another ten hauling himself into the leather.

Finally, he reined the claybank away from the hitchrack. Slouched low in his saddle, he booted the horse eastward, past the shopkeepers and townsmen who ventured back onto the boardwalk, muttering and exclaiming at the carnage.

"Don't let me catch you in town again, Falcon!" the marshal called from the broken window.

As the horse and rider disappeared down the far end of the street, trailing a brown dust plume, Longarm frowned up at the window as the marshal pulled his head back inside. Boots pounded the floorboards, descended the stairs, crossed the saloon's main hall. The marshal looked out the first story's broken window, stepped over the casing and into the street.

Longarm poked his hat brim back off his forehead, staring in amazement.

He'd thought the lawman had spoken in a strangely high voice. Now he saw why.

The town marshal of Diamondback shoved the flaps of her jacket back and planted her fists on her hips, a healthy set of breasts pushing at her loosely woven blouse, the first three buttons of which were undone, and the lacy chemise beneath, like two baby pigs trying to shove their way out of a croaker sack.

When she finished surveying the human wreckage which Longarm had left sprawled in the street, she sauntered over to him and stared up at him from beneath the narrow brim of her olive plainsman, causing Longarm's heart to skip a beat.

Diamondback's town marshal had not only an amazing set of tits, she had one of the three or four most beautiful, blue-eyed faces he'd ever seen—strong-jawed, straight-nosed, with high, chiseled cheekbones and a small beauty mark on her neck.

She was a big-boned woman, athletic-looking and tan. She was well curved and full-hipped, but Longarm doubted she wore one extra pound on her beguiling frame. Her long, straight, straw-colored hair winged out slightly from both sides of her face, the olive skin glistening slightly with sweat.

She offered a lopsided smile, full lips stretching back from white teeth, the right eyetooth protruding alluringly. "Thanks for the help. You the federal from Denver?"

Longarm's voice caught in his throat. "Yep."

"Come on," said Marshal Blassingame, reaching into Longarm's shirt pocket and plucking out a three-for-a-nickel cheroot.

She stuck the cigar in her teeth, beckoned with her eyes, and mounted the saloon's front porch. "The poison's on me."

Chapter 4

Longarm followed the rangy marshal through the batwings, admiring the subtle sway of her round ass under the tight denim trousers, and her slow, regal stride. The top of the barman's head and eyes appeared, peeking up from the other side of the bar. The eyes slid from Marshal Blassingame to Longarm, then back to the marshal.

The man straightened, his fleshy, round, hairless face flushed crimson. "Jesus Christ, are you two about *done*?"

"For now," the marshal said. "Give me a bottle and two glasses, will you, Jake?"

As the barman grabbed a bottle and two shot glasses off the back bar, he glanced around the saloon, at the bloody bodies, overturned chairs, and smashed tables. Turning, he set the bottle and glasses on the mahogany and ran his piqued gaze across the room once more. "Who's gonna pay for this, Merle?"

"Oh, quit cryin' and check their pockets, Jake. Yesterday was payday out to the Royal Flush." Marshal Blassingame grabbed the bottle by the neck, plucked up the glasses with the first three fingers of her left hand, and glanced at Longarm.

She rolled her eyes with disgust, then strolled over to a

table in the room's shadowy right flank, a good distance from the carnage.

As the barman mumbled and grumbled behind him, Longarm followed her, still dumbfounded by her beauty and position, not to mention her obvious toughness and handiness with a shooting iron.

She kicked out a chair, sagged into it, then popped the cork from the whiskey bottle, and splashed the oily, amber concoction to the rim of each glass. She tilted the bottle's neck up and was about to cork it when, catching him staring, she stopped and hiked a shoulder.

"You were expecting a flat-chested marshal. Put it behind you. We got official business." She replaced the cork in the bottle's mouth, picked up her glass, sagged back in her chair, and stuck Longarm's cigar between her teeth.

She looked at him expectantly. Longarm chuckled, sat down, and plucked a cigar and lucifer from his shirt pocket.

He scratched the match to life on his thumbnail and held it across the table. The marshal leaned forward, staring over the flame, appraising him coolly, as he lit her cigar. She sat back in her chair, blowing smoke at the rafters.

When Longarm had lit his own cheroot, Marshal Blassingame said, "My father was town marshal before a drunk sheepherder shot him last fall. None of these other nancy boys"—she glanced at the bartender, who was grunting and dragging one of the dead men toward the batwings by his ankles—"wanted the job."

"You're right handy with a shootin' iron."

"Never much cared for dolls. You can call me Merle if I can call you . . ."

"Longarm." He shrugged sheepishly and puffed his cheroot. "Everybody does. Long arm of the law or somesuch nonsense. Full handle is Deputy U.S. Marshal Custis Long."

She sat slumped in her chair, nodding as she studied him, her cool eyes curious. "I've heard of you."

"So, what's with these boys, if we can keep digressing from the main topic awhile longer?" Longarm canted his head toward the dead men in the room and on the street. "Why did they want your clock cleaned so bad? Ain't the boys around here been taught how to treat a lady?" He grinned and sipped the whiskey, ignoring how it raked his tonsils before setting an odd fire in his chest.

"That fool Falcon wanted to marry me." She chuffed and threw back her own shot, slammed the glass back onto the table and reached for the bottle.

When she saw Longarm's skeptical glance, she paused, shrugged, and popped the cork. "Oh, I got drunk a couple weeks back and told him I would. I mean, I *guess* I did. I don't recollect. That's what Jake and a couple others told me. Anyway, when I told Falcon I'd had a change of heart, he got all sour and said I had three days to reconsider . . . or else."

She sighed, puffed the cigar, and glanced at the second dead man the bartender was hauling out the door. "I reckon this was his 'or else.'" She chuckled. "He brought his pa's men in from their Royal Flush ranch to give me hell. Couldn't do it himself." She looked pointedly at Longarm, squinting her eyes a little. "Now, what kinda *man* is that?"

Longarm let smoke stream out his nostrils and looked at her from under his brows. "I for one, Merle, would do it myself."

Her cool gaze slid across his chest and shoulders, returned to his eyes. Her upper lip curled. "You reckon you could?"

"I reckon I'd try." His eyes flashed rascally. "And the devil take the hindmost."

She dipped her chin slightly and pursed her lips. She raised her shot glass. "I reckon he would at that."

Longarm raised his own glass, and they both threw back their shots. "Now, then," he said, skidding his glass toward the middle of the table and waving her off when she extended the bottle toward him. "Seems to be the fashion in this country—comely lasses luring men off to their graves. Wanna fill me in?"

Marshal Blassingame refilled her glass. Longarm was not only amazed by how well she handled a six-shooter, but by how well she could hold her hooch. She was on her third shot in five minutes, and her eyes were blue steel.

"Magnusson and his wolf women," Merle said, leaning back and shoving her fingers into her jeans pockets. "That's what we call 'em around here, on account of they have a pet wolf runnin' with 'em. Magnusson's off his nut, and so, apparently, are his daughters."

"When'd they start killin'?"

"About nine months ago. When prospectors started rushing into Diamondback Canyon after a man named Hjelmar Petterson found a nugget in his placer diggings worth four thousand dollars. Magnusson has several cabins up there. Apparently, he got tired of the company, so he and his girls went to work killin' most of the prospectors in their area. Eight men dead in three weeks. A couple witnesses claimed the girls got them to let their guard down, and ole Magnusson went in either shootin' or swinging a pick. They stripped the bodies, took all valuables, and vamoosed."

"They pretty much stick around the Diamondback?"

"Pretty much. Magnusson was one of the first to settle the canyon—him and about three Basque sheepherders—after the French fur trappers disappeared about twenty years ago. His last Indian wife is buried near Skull Pass. I figure that's why he's staying."

She sighed and threw back her shot, gritted her teeth as the coffin varnish hit her stomach. "Good luck finding them. I've been up and down that canyon twice now, and found neither hide nor hair. Magnusson's got about three or four other cabins, some in the Mummy Range, some in the Neversummers. Some claim they've even seen him and those wolf girls as far south as Ute Creek Peak in the Mummy Range. They haul an old teepee around on a travois."

"What about the girls?"

The marshal snorted. "They're pretty . . . and wild."

"Must be something in the water around here."

"And men, bein' men, can't resist 'em. I hope you can resist them, Longarm, cause I hear tell they'll give you a hard-on that'll last a lifetime."

"Business before pleasure," Longarm said, feeling his ears warm at the lass's salty talk. He'd been around farm-talking females before, but none of them filled out their blouses half as well as this gal did. "Both of 'em have Indian blood?"

"Yeah, but only one is dark. The other must've taken after Magnusson's Norski side. She favors a Viking queen." Merle snorted again. "They're quite a pair. If you ever catch sight of 'em, you won't forget 'em. Just don't forget yourself and try to fuck 'em." She clucked and threw back the rest of her drink.

The whiskey was so bad, Longarm decided to have another shot to numb the dull ache this alley-talking looker was setting up in his loins. What was it about pretty women with blue tongues . . . ?

When he'd refilled his shot glass and taken another sip, he grated, "You drink this shit daily?"

She smiled. "Jake claims it has healing properties."

Longarm took another sip and shook his head. "I reckon I don't have anything to heal." He lifted the glass to the window to see if anything solid were floating around in the hooch. "You really think old Magnusson and his wolf women are going to be that hard to track?"

43

"Yep. 'Cause I've tried. The canyon's out of my jurisdiction, but the county sheriff ain't worth puke. I tried, all right, and came up empty."

"A man might have an easier time . . . since it's men they're after."

"Chew that up finer."

"If I was to go up the canyon rigged out like a prospector who aimed to stay awhile . . ."

The marshal stared at him pensively, nodding. "It's worth a try, I reckon. You ever been up that country before?"

"Time or two, but I wouldn't say I know it."

"You'll need a guide."

"Got one in mind?"

"Got one already arranged. My uncle, Comanche John Blassingame. He's been at loose ends lately, needs a job to keep him from drinkin' too much and carousing. He was prospecting up the St. Vrain, but then his diggings dried up."

"How much he charge?"

She hiked a shoulder and tapped ashes from her cigar onto the floor. "Five dollars a day. Uncle Sam can afford that, can't he?"

"That's nepotism, Marshal."

"Sure as shit, Longarm." She glanced out the street-side windows, beyond which several men were laying Falcon's dead gunnies out on the boardwalk before the women's clothing store. "Too late to get started today, though. Besides, Uncle John's sparking a widow lady over to Camp Collins. Won't be back here till late tonight."

She stood and donned her hat, adjusting it atop her head, arranging her hair, taking her time as though to give Longarm a good study of her figure, full breasts pushing at the blouse and the lacy chemise exposed a good two inches beneath the top of her cleavage, nipples prodding the cotton like small buttons.

Though she was a big, healthy-looking girl, she had a proportionately narrow waist and well-turned hips and thighs. Her long legs were the kind that set a man to imagining how they'd feel, wrapped around his waist.

She glanced at Longarm and mashed out her cigar under her boot toe. "Forget it, Deputy. I've had enough trouble with men for one day."

"Nothing to forget, Marshal. I never trifle with wildcats . . . no matter how pretty they are."

She set her hands on the table and leaned toward him, her blouse billowing out from her chest, giving him a bird's-eye view of her cleavage. "Remember that when you go up the canyon tomorrow. It's usually the big, handsome sons of bitches who are especially vulnerable."

She remained leaning over him a stretched second, giving him a good, long look of what she was denying him, then straightened, winked, adjusted her hat, and strolled out the batwings.

"I can't tell if I was just complimented or insulted," Longarm told the barman setting up a table on the other side of the room.

The man stopped, his sun-seared face flushed from exertion, a lock of hair hanging over his sweaty forehead. "Poison. That's what that girl is." He kicked a chair against the table. "Pretty poison."

Longarm stood, donned his hat, and headed for the batwings. His headache was back. He'd take some air and get the lay of the town. "Lot of it around here, ain't there?"

Longarm moseyed around town for a while, though there wasn't much to mosey around but shacks and sagebrush; then he rented a speckle-gray pack mule and packsaddle from the Occidental Livery and Feed Barn.

He purchased miner's garb and a couple of picks and shovels from the mercantile for show, and camping supplies and foodstuffs. With his saddle horse, pack mule, and panniers secured in the livery barn, and a room rented at the Rutherford B. Hayes Hotel at the west edge of town, at the base of an anvil-shaped rimrock, he enjoyed a beer and a surprisingly good steak at a small brick-and-adobe tavern nestled in the cottonwoods along the Diamondback River. The place had been recommended by the livery owner.

Longarm had intended to call it an early day. He and the marshal's uncle would be heading out at first light. Besides, it had been a long train ride from Denver, and, having been otherwise occupied with Cynthia Larimer, he hadn't gotten much sleep the night before.

But before he knew it, he'd become involved shooting craps with a couple of good-humored placer miners, who told him this and that about the river and the canyon he was about to traverse. He didn't wander over to the Hayes until well after ten o'clock, with distant thunder and the smell of rain pushing in from the mountains.

He shucked out of his clothes and crawled into the soft, albeit lumpy bed, and blew out his lamp. He watched lightning flash in the window for about two minutes before the rumbling thunder and the fresh smell of the rain and sage lured him off to slumberland.

He wasn't sure how long he'd been asleep before something woke him.

He opened his eyes and blinked into the darkness. Lightning lit up the two west-facing windows, for half a second filling the room with a cold, violet light.

Just enough light for just enough time for Longarm to see the hatted, jacket-clad figure moving toward him from the door. One flap of the jacket was pulled back behind a holstered revolver.

Chapter 5

Warning bells clanging in his head, Longarm flung his right hand out toward the double-action .44 holstered on the chair back beside the bed.

"Hold on!" a female voice hissed, so drowned by a sudden thunderclap that Longarm was slow to comprehend.

In an eyeblink, his pistol was in his hand, cocked, and aimed at the intruder's belly. The intruder aimed a silver-plated Colt at Longarm.

"It's Merle," she said, keeping her voice low.

"Christalmighty!" Longarm groused, still too shocked to release his grip on his .44. "What the hell you think you're doin'?"

She stood about five feet from the bed. He could see only her silhouette during lightning flashes. Rain pelted the windows, and the wind was kicking up.

"You holster yours," she said, voice like steel, "I'll holster mine."

Longarm wasn't in the habit of dropping his own gun when another was being aimed at him—even when that other gun was held by a blond heart-stopper like Merle Blassingame.

"You first," Longarm countered.

47

"We'll do it together."

"On the count of three."

Merle said, "One, two, three . . ."

Neither gun moved a hair.

"Oh, for Pete's sake!" she said, giving her silver-plated Navy a twirl and dropping it into its holster. "I came to fuck, not swap lead."

Longarm let his Colt sag. "Huh?"

She doffed her hat, slung it toward a chair in the far corner, then began unbuckling her cartridge belt. When she had the belt off and was slinging it over the same chair holding Longarm's belt and holster, he reached over toward the chair himself and, keeping his eyes on the girl, dropped his .44 in its sheath.

He watched, by intermittent lightning flashes, thunder rumbling and rattling the windows, as Merle unbuttoned her shirt quickly, shrugged out of the loose-woven garment and her deerskin jacket, and tossed both in the general direction of her hat.

"Mind if I light a lamp? I like to see what I'm gettin' into."

Longarm swallowed. "Right practical."

When she'd lit the lamp on the dresser, she kicked out of her boots and did a cobra imitation, wiggling out of her jeans and men's skintight longhandles, then hopping around, full breasts jouncing beneath a lacy chemise, as she pulled off her men's white socks.

Finally, naked from the waist down, she stepped up to the bed, regarded Longarm wistfully from between the mussed wings of her long, blond hair, which the wan lamplight caressed lovingly.

She crossed her arms and lifted the sheer chemise toward her neck. The material raked over her breasts, catching on the nipples, jostling them slightly before she pulled the garment up over her head. Her hair rose with the chemise and fell back down across her shoulders, sticking

48

out here and there like straw from a shock, several strands framing the big, round, pink-nippled globes of her breasts.

Assuming a mock bullfighter's stance, she held the chamise out between the thumb and index finger of her left hand, as though it were a cape, then dropped it straight down to the floor. She tossed her hair out, giving Longarm an uncluttered view of her body.

Her belly was flat, the hips nicely rounded, and the thighs arcing in a long, graceful curve—the hard, toned thighs of a woman who spent a lot of time on horseback.

"You like?" she said.

Longarm swallowed. His heart was thudding like a Ute war drum. He always slept in his birthday suit, and his shaft was tenting the single blanket he'd drawn up to his waist.

She reached down—"Christ, is that another .44 under there?"—and wrapped her hand around his cock as though around the neck of a chicken she were about to strangle for supper.

Longarm's stomach lurched as though he'd been shot out of a cannon.

He grabbed her wrist, pulled her down to him, and kissed her. She sagged against him and opened her lips, ramming her tongue into his mouth and squirming against him, her feet still on the floor.

Kissing her, he wrapped his left arm around her shoulders and, sliding to one side, began pulling her onto the bed.

She pulled her tongue back into her mouth and smiled while pressing her lips to his. "I wanna be on top."

"Why doesn't that surprise me?"

Longarm squeezed her arm, pulling her close while he kissed her, enjoying her warm, full lips against his. Then he lay back and threw aside the covers, exposing his fully erect, throbbing shaft which a sudden lightning flash illuminated dramatically.

She groaned like a bitch in heat and straddled him,

49

thunder clapping and making the entire building shudder, while the wind blasted the walls and windows with heavy rain.

She kissed him and ran her hands down his arms and across the hard bulging slabs of his chest. Suddenly she looked down at him, her eyes meeting his. "I don't visit the room of every handsome stranger who rides into town, I want you to know."

He pinched her nipples between his thumbs and index fingers, his thick mustache turning up with a grin. "To what do I owe the honor?"

"I reckon you saved my life. I was outgunned."

"I have a feelin' you'd have figured a way to save your bacon."

"Doubt it. Some of Falcon's boys were gunslicks from Texsas and Oklahoma. His daddy, ole Amos Falcon himself, hired 'em to keep squatters off his spread." She scooted down his thighs then leaned forward until her hair was dropping down over Longarm's groin, making his whole being tingle.

"No sir," she cooed as the lightning flashed and the thunder clapped, the guttering lamplight sliding shadows to and fro, "I'd be pushing up daisies now if it hadn't been for you, Longarm." She took his shaft in one hand, wrapping her fingers around it, and kissed the head.

"Oh well . . . I reckon there's no point in arguin'." He groaned as she suddenly slid her lips quickly down the length of his shaft, until his head met the back of her opening and closing throat.

He bunched the sheets in his hands and curled his toes as she whipped her lips back up the length of his iron-hard cock, over the circumcised head and off with a slight popping sound.

She scooted back up his thighs, until her hip bones lay over his. She pushed up on her knees and guided the head of his shaft into her furred slot, then slowly slid down upon him, the shaft rising into the hot, wet core of her.

Her voice was graveled and breathy. "Thank you, Custis." She rose up and down, shuddering as if chilled to the bone, her hair tumbling around her shoulders. "It's all right if I call you Custis, isn't it?"

"Ma'am," Longarm grunted as she began rising and falling faster, his fingertips digging into her waist just above her hipbones, "you can call me anything you want."

"Merle."

"Huh?" She was fairly bouncing atop him now, the bed springs squawking, the headboard tapping the wall.

"Call me Merle."

She stopped suddenly and looked down at him seriously again, her round, sweat-slick breasts flattened on his chest.

She lowered her lips to his, chewed his lower lip for a second, then lifted her head again and ran her hand brusquely through his hair. "But only here. Out there, I'm Marshal Blassingame to you, chump, and everyone else."

"Why not, since you ask so nice?" Longarm winced, his shaft standing tall inside her, waiting, his heart threatening to blow blood out his ears. "Now, you mind if we save the rest of the chitchat for later?"

She began thrusting her hips again, rising up and down on her haunches. It wasn't long before the bed was complaining like a sawyer's two-man timber saw and Merle was groaning and sighing and Longarm was grunting and gritting his teeth as the storm blasted away outside like a night skirmish during the Little Misunderstanding Between the States.

Longarm held himself back for as long as he could, grinding his teeth and digging his fingers into her hips. Finally, he threw his head back, arched his back, and let go.

"Gawd!" the marshal cried, grinding down hard and throwing her own head back on her shoulders, stretching her lips back from her teeth and hissing like a wildcat.

It took about five minutes for them both to catch their breath.

"Christ," Merle said, looking at him from the bed's second pillow, her hair half-covering her face in the lightning flashes. She was shaking her head from side to side.

Longarm chuckled. "I gotta say, Merle," he said, reaching over and squeezing her sweat-damp thigh, "it's been a while since I've been put up that wet my ownself."

It was a lie. Cynthia Larimer had pleased him like few other women could, but there was something about having a big, athletic fillie like Merle Blassingame hauling your ashes, with her two good handfuls of bobbing tits assaulting your face while she did it.

That and the fact she'd obviously been so starved for it.

She kept her voice low. "I hope no one heard. I reckon it's not professional—the town marshal fuckin' a federal lawman here on official business."

"Life's too short not to throw out the book a time or two."

Longarm crawled out of bed and grabbed one of his cheroots off the dresser. Standing naked before the dresser, facing the bed, letting the cool, fresh air dry the sweat from his skin, he snapped a lucifer to life and touched the flame to the cigar's tip, puffing smoke.

Rain tapped against the windows, weaker than before.

"How in the hell did you get in here, anyway? I know I locked the door. As many times as bad folks have tried perforatin' my hide to avenge themselves or family members, it's become an obsession with me." He blew out the match and tossed it into an ashtray atop the dresser.

"I live just down the hall," Merle said, propping her head on one elbow and regarding him in the sliding shadows. "And old Grassley saw fit to provide me with a skeleton key." She patted the bed. "Come back, Custis." She gave a catlike groan. "I wanna do it some more."

"Already?"

"I ain't had it in a long time."

"What about Falcon?"

"That don't count. I was drunk."

"I should get some sleep. I gotta long ride ahead of me."

Even in the near darkness he could see her pooch her lips out. "Pleeeeeease?"

Longarm padded back to the bed. He sat on the edge and stared down at her rounded hips, the hard thighs curled together as she reclined on her right side, head propped on an elbow. He sighed.

She was just too good to pass up. Besides, he had no idea how long it would be before he'd have it again, heading into the tall and uncut like he was.

The heavy globes of her breasts were mashed together as they slanted toward the rumpled sheets. Her skin glistened faintly in the wan lamplight and the purple glow slanting through the window, between the lightning strikes that seemed to be dwindling as the storm moved on.

She reached up, plucked the cigar from between his fingers, leaned back, and took a deep drag. Her breasts flattened slightly against her chest, shaded nipples pointing toward the ceiling. As she exhaled the smoke straight up, Longarm took the cigar back and set it on the washstand beside the bed, with the coal hanging over the edge; then he leaned down and nuzzled her breasts.

"Duty calls, I reckon."

She chuckled, rolling onto her back and spreading her knees, and ran her hands threw his hair. "Jesus, you fuck good, Custis!"

At the same time, in the dark, wet alley behind the hotel, two men were hunkered down on their knees beside the privy, staring up at the single lighted window on the hotel's second story.

It was the room from which they'd been hearing the muffled sounds of rapturous lovemaking and in which they'd been watching the girl's long-haired silhouette bouncing up and down in the window. The tall gent had gotten out of bed for something and returned, and the sounds of lovemaking had resumed, but this time there wasn't anything to see as the man was on top and they were both below the window line.

The man with the black hat and black sideburns framing his broad, harsh face nudged the other man, who was slightly shorter, with a large, hard gut and greasy red hair spilling down from his cream plainsman. The black-haired hombre jerked his head toward the front of the hotel. The red-haired gent nodded and hefted his double-barreled Greener in both hands across his thick chest.

The black-haired gent quietly raked a shell into the breech of his Henry rifle and straightened. With a last cautious glance at the window from which passionate sighs and groans emanated, above the wet ticks of the raindrops dripping off the roof of the hotel and the privy, he moved off at an angle toward Diamondback's main street.

The red-haired gent followed, taking quick, mincing steps with his stubby legs, his small, booted feet making sucking sounds in the mud.

They tried to avoid the largest puddles as they approached the hotel's west front corner and mounted the boardwalk. As the black-haired gent reached for the front door, a face appeared in the shadows on the other side of the building, at the far end of the boardwalk.

The black-haired gent stopped suddenly, turning his head and tensing.

The figure walked into the light emanating from the curtained front window, upon which gold-leaf letters formed the words "THE RUTHERFORD B. HAYES HOTEL." The third man was tall and lanky in his spruce green duster and bowler hat, a long, thin cheroot protruding from between his teeth.

He held a sawed-off ten-gauge in one hand, a Buntline

Special in the other. A grin twisted his lips around the cheroot.

"Gonna get yourself shot, Pyle, you son of a bitch," the black-haired gent said.

"Try it someday, Giff. I want you to."

"Shut-up, both of yas!" intervened the red-haired hombre, who's name was Sloan, as he stepped between them both and opened the hotel's front door. "We got a job to do, and I'm thirsty."

As the men stepped inside the hotel's small, carpeted lobby, where a fire smoked in the hearth, they turned to the front desk at the right side of the room. A birdlike woman with a tight cap of red gray curls and small, round spectacles sat behind the desk, reading a Bible spread open before her, beside the hotel register, a pen, and an ink bottle.

She was shaking her head, lips pursed with disgust.

As the three men approached the desk, she placed a finger on the page she'd been reading, to hold her place, and looked up.

As her eyes took in the three gun-packing hard cases before her, her hazel eyes sharpened and her paper white cheeks colored.

The squawking of the bed upstairs could be heard as if from far away, the ceiling timbers complaining faintly, the chandelier at the base of the stairs jostling, the cylinders chiming.

Sloan smiled, his small eyes slanting wickedly, as he aimed his shotgun at the woman's sparrow chest, her pointy nubbin breasts pushing at her black, lace-edged shirtwaist. "Key for the room where the, uh"—he jerked his head toward the staircase flanking the desk— "*entertainin's* goin' on."

Chapter 6

The birdlike woman gasped and jerked back in her chair. Her eyes rose from the twin barrels yawning at her spindly bosom, and her nostrils flared angrily. "Appears the devil is having a high old time in town tonight."

A muffled squeal rose from the top of the stairs.

Sloan narrowed his steel blue eyes even more, his plump, freckled cheeks balling humorously. On the other side of the black-haired gent called Giff, the tall man, Pyle, said, "Lady, you ain't seen nothin' yet."

Sloan snapped his fingers. "Hand over the key."

The woman swallowed, eyes twitching fearfully, one hand spread upon her chest. "I . . . I believe the marshal is in there."

Giff bounded forward, bellying up to the counter and reaching across to grab the old woman by the front of her shirtwaist, jerking her bony face up close to his. He bunched his lips and spoke through gritted teeth, keeping his voice down.

"Lady, hand over the fuckin' key, or I'm gonna drill an extra hole in your ugly face. Got it?"

Her eyes bulged. Her mouth formed a thin, downward-curving slash.

Moving only her hand, she reached under the desk, feeling around blindly, making a soft clanking noise, before finally setting a black key on the desk. To the key was attached a round metal plate engraved with the number 12.

Giff dropped his gaze to the key. Still clutching the woman's dress, keeping her face six inches from his, he said, "Now, do we need to hogtie you and cut out your tongue, or you gonna be a good ugly bitch and stay right here behind this desk . . . with your fucking mouth *shut*?"

Her small voice shook. "Amos Falcon sent you, didn't he? On account of what"—she glanced at the ceiling near the stairs—"the marshal done to his son."

"That wasn't the answer I was lookin' for."

"Oh, Lordy," the woman chirped, tears squeezing out her eyes and dribbling down her pasty cheeks. "Yes . . . I'll stay here and be quiet. Please don't hurt me!"

"If your old man comes snoopin' around, you keep him here, too, understand?"

The woman jerked her head up and down.

Giff tossed her back against the cubbyholes built into the back wall. He turned, glanced darkly at Sloan and Pyle, and headed for the stairs.

With Sloan and Pyle following in a shaggy line, Giff took the stairs quietly, two steps at a time, on the balls of his feet. Sloan tried doing the same, but his legs were too short, so he took only one step at a time. Long-legged Pyle scowled behind him as he followed the stocky redhead, having to move more slowly than he was comfortable with.

As Giff approached the top of the stairs, the groans and the bed squawks got louder.

He set his left boot down on the third step from the top. It squeaked like a baby bird fallen from its nest. He froze, gritting his teeth, pricking his ears to listen.

The bed squawks and the passionate sounds of lovemaking continued without pause. Giff smiled. He turned to the others, shook his head with relief, indicated the loose step with his rifle barrel, then stepped up and over it to the top of the stairs.

As the men stole quietly down the hall, the bedsprings went *shee-saw*, *shee-saw*, *shee-saw*, while the man grunted and cursed. Beneath the man's low exclamations, the girl groaned and sighed.

"Oh, god, Custis . . . oh . . . Jesus *Christ*!"

Giff glanced at Sloan slightly flanking him on his right, and smiled crookedly. They stopped before the door, Pyle behind them, a full head taller. Giff reached for the doorknob, then stopped. The door wasn't quite latched.

"Oh, Christ, you fuck soooo good, Custis!" fairly shouted the marshal above the bed's sawing and the man's grunting and cursing.

Pyle snorted softly and whispered. "Sometimes this job is just too easy."

Giff motioned for the other two men to crab out beside him. At the same time, he took two steps straight back, holding the rifle in his right hand, aimed at the door's center. He raised his left foot and, swinging his left arm out for balance, slammed his boot against the door, just left of the knob.

The door banged back against the wall with a thunderous boom, making the whole room jump. Giff grinned wolfishly and shouted, "Message from Amos Falcon, Marshal!" He took two long strides into the lantern-lit room and aimed the rifle with both hands at the bed.

He froze before he could get the barn-blaster's stock leveled. His eyes nearly popped out of their sockets.

On the bed before him stood Marshal Blassingame in all her butt-naked splendor. She'd just risen three feet above the bed, yellow hair and big, round tits rising then falling as her feet plunged back toward the rumpled sheets below.

She grinned, eyes bright, as she raised a Winchester straight out from her belly.

Giff's lower jaw sagged as he brought the rifle to bear. "Shit."

Before he could pull the trigger, the marshal's Winchester's stabbed smoke and flames, the shot sounding like crashing boulders in the close quarters.

In his balbriggans and hat, double-action Colt extended in his right hand, Longarm had crouched in front of the dresser. He'd glimpsed two shadows hunkered by the privy when he'd gotten out of bed to light a cigar.

Now, Merle's first shot slammed into the black-haired gent with the Henry rifle. Screaming, the man stumbled straight back toward the door, triggering both rifle barrels into the ceiling over the bed.

The twin blasts rocked the entire building, plaster and wood raining onto the bed in front of Diamondback's naked marshal, who quickly recocked her Winchester.

Longarm squeezed his Colt's trigger a half second after Merle had fired her Winchester, his own slug drilling the man through his right arm. The man fell back into a short, fat gent with long, red hair and wielding a double-barreled Greener. The red-haired gent threw the black-haired hombre to one side, stepped forward, and began raising his Greener.

Longarm and Marshal Blassingame fired at the same time, the shots ripping through the man's lumpy chest.

He screamed, mouth forming a horseshoe-sized O as he stumbled back, tripping over the black-haired gent and slamming against the wall on the other side of the hall. He continued shrieking while trying to raise the carbine.

Longarm and Merle pumped two more shots into his chest and belly. Blood spurting from the holes and spraying the papered wall behind him, he dropped the Greener and staggered sideways, stumbling out of Longarm's view behind the wall right of the open door.

A loud thump said he'd fallen at the same time that the tall gent in the bowler and duster leaped behind the wall on the left side of the door. The tall man snaked a sawed-off ten-gauge around the door latch and settled the barrels on Merle.

Longarm drilled a round into the door casing, but the rider held the shotgun steady.

Both barrels of the gut-shredder exploded.

To Longarm's right, Merle leaped in a long, high arc off the bed's right side as the double-ought buck sliced the air where she'd been standing and blew two horse collar–sized holes in the plastered wall at the head of the bed.

Longarm fired another round, then Merle fired four in a straight line along the wall left of the door. The shotgunner screamed, staying out of sight behind the wall. Longarm triggered his pistol from one knee, then ducked as a long, silver-plated revolver barrel snaked around the door frame and popped twice.

Longarm threw himself forward and lay belly-flat as a slug shattered a window behind him while another barked through a metal handle on the dresser.

The shooter bellowed with anger and pain. Then, as Longarm thumbed open his empty Colt's loading gate, the man dashed past the door, clamping his left hand, which also held the Buntline Special, to his bloody right shoulder. He disappeared past the wall, boots pounding the floorboards.

"Goddamnit, I'm out!" Longarm barked.

"Me, too," Merle shouted from the other side of the bed. She tossed Longarm's Winchester onto the bed, then leaped onto the bed herself, running toward the chair over which her shell belt hung. "Don't you federals keep your long guns loaded?"

"As poor as you're shootin' tonight, sweetheart, I reckon next time I better get ya a damn *Gatling* gun!" Longarm knocked the spent shells from his Colt's cylinder then reached toward his cartridge belt.

"Poor as *I'm* shooting? What were you aiming at—the *wall*? Here!" Kneeling at the edge of the bed, breasts dipping toward the floor, Merle tossed her own Colt toward Longarm.

He caught the revolver and flipped it so the grips were in his palm. "I reckon bein' half-naked fouled my aim." He tossed his own empty Colt onto the bed and ran out the door.

"Finish that son of a bitch!" Merle shouted behind him.

"What the hell you think I'm doin'—goin' out for a smoke?" Longarm grumbled, sprinting barefoot down the hall toward the stairs, pistol held straight up in his right hand, balbriggans stretched taut across his chest and thighs.

On the first floor, a woman screamed. A man shouted.

Longarm dashed down the stairs two steps at a time, into the pale, buttery light shed by the chandelier at the bottom of the stairs and from lamps in the lobby to the right.

When he was half-down, a gun barked. The slug chewed into the railing before him, peppering his balbriggans with wooden shards and splinters.

Longarm ducked and extended his pistol over the railing.

"I'll kill her!" the tall hombre in the bowler and duster shouted, eyes bright with fury as he held the wife of the hotel's proprieter before him, one arm around her neck.

She flopped before him like a rag doll, gagging as he drew his forearm taught against her throat and snugged the end of the Buntline Special against her temple.

"Throw the gun down, you federal son of a bitch, or I'll blow this bitch's brains all over this lobby."

Longarm never wore his badge unless he was arresting someone, but after the saloon shootings word must have somehow gotten out that he was a lawman.

A foolproof way of getting turned down with a shovel was giving up your weapon to a badman. Longarm made as if he were about to drop the revolver over the railing, then gripped it once more, took hasty aim at the tall man's head jutting over the hotelier's wife, and fired.

61

The hotelman's wife screamed and the tall man bellowed as the slug sliced his left ear sticking out from beneath his bowler's frayed brim. He released the woman and staggered back, dropping to one knee and facing the door, cursing loudly.

The woman was on her knees between the man and Longarm, clutching one hand to her battered throat and gagging, her eyes bulging.

"Get the hell outta the way!" Longarm shouted, waving his arm.

"Ohhhh!" the woman sobbed and threw herself right, crabbing toward the gap between the wall and the lobby's front desk.

Longarm squeezed off another shot, but the man crawled around the far side of the front desk, and Longarm's shot plunked into an upholstered chair behind him.

The man snaked his silver-plated pistol around the end of the desk and fired. The slug barked into a rail pillar to Longarm's right.

He fired again quickly.

Longarm ducked. His right knee slipped off the step.

He reached for the rail, missed it, and a half second later found himself tumbling down the stairs, the stairwell spinning around him and setting up a high ringing in his ears.

He rolled to a sudden halt against the wall at the bottom landing and jerked a look toward the lobby.

Grinning while holding one hand to his bloody ear, the blood dribbling in three separate streaks down his neck and onto his duster's collar, the tall gent scuttled toward Longarm on his hands and knees.

He whooped for joy and raised the pistol.

The old woman bolted suddenly out from the gap behind the desk, raising what appeared to be a hide-wrapped bung-starter in her right hand.

Screaming, she slammed the mallet down hard on the tall gent's pistol. He wailed and triggered the pistol into the floor before dropping the gun and removing his hand from his ear to clutch his arm.

"You fucking *bitch*!" the man screamed.

"Die, bastard, die!" she shrieked, bringing the mallet down once more across his shoulder, then laying it flat against his head. It made a dull cracking sound.

"To hell with you . . . threatening a defenseless lady when her husband's off fishin'!"

Longarm had gained his knees and was trying to draw a bead on the would-be assassin again, but the woman was in the way, pummeling the gent with the bung-starter. The man screamed and cursed and crawled back toward the door, the old lady following him and berating him with both words and the hide-wrapped mallet, the whacks *resounding* across the lobby.

"Get out," she screamed in rage. "Get out! Get out! Get out!"

Longarm gained his feet and ran around the front desk. The tall gent had the door open. Raising his left arm to shield the old woman's blows, he bolted through the opening and jerked the door closed behind him.

"Lady, get outta the way!" Longarm shouted, shoving her against the desk then slipping outside.

He dropped to one knee on the hotel's stoop and peered into the darkness, the mud puddles in the street before him glistening blue starlight.

The tall gent stumbled off across the street, angling to Longarm's right, one hand to his ear.

A small shadow shot out from the direction of the livery barn, growling and yipping, and digging its teeth into the man's right calf.

"Hold it, you son of a bitch!" Merle shouted from somewhere above Longarm. The porch roof impeded his view.

As the dog clutched the man's leg, growling and shaking its head, the man kicked at it. Unable to dislodge the stalwart little beast, he turned toward the hotel.

Something flashed dully in his right hand.

He kicked at the dog again, still unable to free himself. The dog did a bizarre pirouette on its back legs as the man swung it in a circle, cursing it. Beneath the little dog's steady, vibrating growls, there was the sound of a pistol hammer cocking.

Longarm extended the Colt and fired. One beat later, Merle fired above him, the rifle shot ringing out across the town and echoing hollowly. As the tall man jerked, Longarm fired two more rounds at nearly the same time that Merle fired three more from Longarm's rifle.

The tall man flew straight back, howling and triggering his revolver skyward. He landed on his back in the mud with a dull splash.

The little dog squealed and ran off into the shadows on the other side of the street.

Longarm stood and stepped off the stoop, lowering his revolver and peering up over his right shoulder. On a narrow balcony with a door standing wide behind her, Merle stood in a hat, longhandles, and boots, still aiming the smoking Winchester at the tall gent sprawled in the mud.

"I think we got him," Longarm said.

Chapter 7

Longarm woke the next morning to the marshal of Diamondback's naked breasts pressed against his back and one long, creamy thigh scissored between his legs.

He'd have gone for a morning romp, as it was early still, the first flush of dawn barely pearling the windows, but when he stirred, Merle merely rolled over and drew the blankets up to her neck, groaning as she drifted back toward sleep.

"Think I'm gonna snore some more," she muttered. "Big day yesterday. You'll probably find Comanche John over to the German Café. You two be careful up there in that canyon. Don't fall prey to any big-titted damsels in distress."

Longarm dropped his legs to the floor and was about to respond, when she stirred once again.

"If you see Mrs. Grassley, tell her she better not spread it around that you and me spent the night together or I'll set the ball rolling about her and the preacher's wife swimming naked in the river together."

With that, she snuggled down under the covers. Within seconds, her breaths were long and regular.

Longarm snorted, rose, and took a whore's bath at the

washstand. He didn't bother to shave, as most prospectors went around with furred jaws, and it was a prospector he'd be impersonating up canyon.

When he'd dressed in his miner's denims, green wool shirt, red neckerchief, sheepskin vest, and the battered plainsman hat he'd bought secondhand, he wrapped his Colt around his lean waist and gathered his saddlebags and rifle.

He leaned down and planted a long kiss on Merle's warm, butter-smooth cheek. She groaned and turned her head to kiss his lips. "Good-bye, Custis. Hurry back."

She chuckled and settled her head back down against the pillow.

Longarm glanced at the full-bodied, big-breasted form beneath the sheets and quilt, and the blond hair cascading over the pillow, and shook his head. "Don't you worry, Marshal. No, sir . . ."

With that, he snugged the covers up around her neck, hiked the saddlebags over his left shoulder, and slipped out of the room. Glancing at the dark bloodstains on the wall and floor, and the bullet holes in the wall and door, he plucked a cheroot from his shirt pocket, stuck it between his lips without lighting it, and headed down the stairs.

Halfway down, he noted the bullet-chewed stair rail.

Since the shooters had been after Merle instead of him, the damage couldn't be construed as federal, and for that he was glad. He hated having to fill out pay vouchers every time he discharged his firearm, and then having to justify each voucher to Billy with that typewriter-playing weasel Henry staring at him reprovingly over his spectacles.

No, compensation for last night's fandango would be up to the Diamondback City Council.

Longarm had hoped in vain to get out of the place without seeing Mrs. Grassley. The henlike, curly-haired woman was on her hands and knees in the lobby, scrubbing the rug in front of the door.

"Blood of the devil," she remarked, glancing up at Longarm, mouth pinched like a puckered asshole. "That must be why it's so hard to get it up!"

Longarm sidled on past her and reached for the door, sucking on his unlit cigar. "That must be it."

"The devil's goin's-on around here," she wheezed, "and I don't just mean the shootin', neither!"

Longarm chuckled. He opened the door and was about to step out, when he remembered Merle's instructions. He looked around the half-open door at the persnickety old woman staring up at him owl-eyed. "Merle mentioned as how she could keep a secret if you could. Um . . . you and the preacher's wife, that is . . ."

He left the woman kneeling there in the foyer, the blood draining out of her face, and headed outside, shivering a little in the early morning chill and hitching the saddlebags higher on his shoulder. The air still smelled like sage and rain. He peered into the cool purple shadows, the false fronts of Diamondback's main drag rearing back against the violet sky, in which a couple of stars still sparkled faintly.

About fifty yards to his left, a white shingle with black letters forming the words "GERMAN CAFÉ" hung over a narrow boardwalk. Smoke streamed from the stone chimney jutting up from the log hovel's shake roof. That and one lone horse hanging its head before a hophouse to Longarm's right were the only signs of life so far.

Longarm fired a match on his thumbnail, lit the cheroot, tossed the match into a mud puddle lingering from last night's gully washer, and angled toward the restaurant, weaving around more puddles.

He was only halfway to the restaurant when a woman's boisterous laugh rang out from inside the hovel's log walls. Adjusting his saddlebags and saddle on his shoulder, and taking another deep drag off the cheroot in his teeth, he pushed through the timbered door, nudging the door back with his Winchester's barrel, and looked around.

Before him was a small, smoky, earthen-floored room, the smell of bacon and heavily spiced sausage wafting on the pine smoke. There were three long wooden tables shrouded in oilcloth and trimmed with fresh-cut flowers poking up from glass vases of various fashions—the only color in the room.

In a rocking chair near the woodstove in the middle of the room, flanked by a wood box, kindling crate, and a stack of yellowed newspapers, a big man in buckskins sat with a chubby brunette in his lap. The woman appeared in her mid-to-late twenties, her rich hair piled atop her head, pale, fleshy cheeks flushed with exertion, brown eyes sparkling as she smiled.

The big man was nuzzling her neck and hefting her breasts through her sackcloth dress, the big orbs the size of watermelons in his roast-sized paws. The woman was half-heartedly struggling against him, laughing and kicking her legs, the hem of her dress and bloodstained apron fluttering around her thick, pantaloon-clad shins and stout black shoes.

"You a very bat old dog, Comanche John!" she scolded, her German accent thick enough to pummel stone. "Look vhere your hands are! That's very bat boy! Very bat—!"

Her eyes discovered Longarm standing in the open doorway, regarding her and the big man wrly, and she quickly feigned an angry expression. "You very bat man, Comanche John! Keeping a girl from her vork!" She planted her feet on the hard-packed floor and wrestled away from the guffawing gent in buckskins. "Vhat if I report you to your niece the marshal, and she *throw* you in chail?"

Comanche John sobered a little, as well, a wry expression stealing over his single lake blue eye, contrasting with his thin gray beard as he grimly studied Longarm. "As trigger-happy as ole Merle has gotten of late, she'd just drill me to save on her feed bill."

The brunette had gained her feet and turned to Longarm. She smoothed her apron over her heaving bosom with one hand and patted her hair with the other, blushing as she smiled demurely at the lawman. "Goot morgan. You are here for to eat?"

"Don't fall all over yourself, Greta," said Comanche John, adjusting the eyepatch over his left eye socket, which was spoked with knife scars and gave his face a ghoulish aspect. "That's the federal I was talking about. Those boys have ice in their veins. They don't trifle with café girls—not when they're on a job, they don't. Bring us both a plate of your best surroundin's. I'll have a glass of goat milk with mine." He touched his flat belly through his buckskin shirt, the wang strings on his beaded elk-hide vest jostling. "You done riled me, set my gut to burnin' . . ."

"Coffee for me," Longarm told Greta, dropping his leather on the nearest bench and leaning his Winchester against the table. He added with a grin around the cheroot in his teeth, "And, while Comanche John done pegged me correct for a federal, I don't have all that much ice in my veins, and I list trifling with café girls as one of my better vices."

"Oh!" the girl cooed, her facing turning red as a western sunset.

She wrinkled her nose at Comanche John then wheeled, skirt and apron tails fluttering about her broad butt and thick legs, and disappeared through a curtained door behind the pine-plank bar.

Longarm stood studying the big, buckskin-clad gent from across the table. He plucked the cheroot from his teeth. "So you be Comanche John. Can't say you favor your niece overmuch."

Comanche John guffawed and struggled up out of the rocker, rising nearly to Longarm's height—a big, slab-chested, flat-bellied, bull-legged gent who looked as though he'd been carved from knotted hickory. As the gray window light angled across him, Longarm saw that he bore the hacked-up stub of an ear on the same side as his deer-hide eye patch.

"Nah, she don't favor me much," said Comanche John, moving toward Longarm, lips stretched back from a surprisingly full set of white teeth. "Poor girl got hit with the ugly stick, she did!"

He wheezed another laugh and thrust his broad hand across the table. "Longarm, a pleasure. I done heared a lot about you. And it just happens to be your good fortune that the man with the most knowledge of the canyon country just happened to be in these very environs when you needed him the most!"

"Know a lot about the canyon, do you?" Longarm said, lowering himself to the bench.

"Shit, I was born and raised in that goddamn canyon. Me and Merle's pa." Comanche John lifted his legs over the bench across the table from Longarm, and sat down, wincing as though from creaky bones.

"Our old man was a fur trapper. We took to raisin' beef when the beaver trade pinched out. We lived up Ute Draw with a dozen scrubs, barely scratched out a livin'. Wasn't good beef country, don't you know. Too easy to lose the critters in them cuts and draws, not to mention to painters, Basque sheepmen, and Utes. I lit out when I was fourteen, joined the cavalry."

He eased the eye patch back and forth across his empty eye socket, scratching an itch. "Comanches done this to my face. That's why white folks call me Comanche John." He jutted his lantern jaw and knobby chin toward Longarm. "You know what the Comanches call me?"

"What's that?"

"One-eyed Hell-spawn!" Comanche John threw his head back on his shoulders and howled. "That's what they started callin' me *after* I healed up and took my revenge!" He plucked a necklace out from under his shirt—a braided rawhide thong with five of what looked like large, dried plums strung through it. "And you know what these here are?"

"What're those, Comanche John?"

"The balls of them Comanches that made off with my eye and my ear!" He loosed another, louder howl, making Longarm's eardrums rattle and a nearby dog start barking. "Pretty fair trade, don't you think?"

"I'd say they got the short end of the stick," Longarm said, as Greta came out of the kitchen with a cup of coffee in one hand, a glass of buttermilk in the other.

"Greta, I ever tell you that story?" Comanche John asked, swatting the woman's broad butt as she wheeled snootily, chin high, and headed back toward the kitchen.

Walking away, she turned her head to call behind her, "Only about feefteen time this year!"

Comanche John snorted. "Woman's crazy for me."

"That's plain to see." Longarm sipped the coffee, piping hot and tar-black, just like he liked it. "So tell me, Comanche John, have you had any run-ins with this Magnusson feller and his wolf women?"

Comanche John shook his head and slurped at his goat milk, licking the white liquid from his mustache. Setting the glass down, he said, "Ain't seen old Magnus in six, seven years. He always did keep to himself—him and his squaws. Heard he had a son once, too, but the boy took sick and died.

"Last time I seen Magnus, I was passin' through the home country on the way to Lulu City, helpin' out a bounty hunter I knew in the cavalry. We stopped for a beer at a little watering hole midway up canyon, and Magnus was there with his daughters, tradin' hides for sugar and flour."

Comanche John snorted and took another sip of the thick milk, lapping again at his whiskers like an old dog. "Even then those two girls were cute as speckled pups. Long-legged, pretty-faced, with titties already pushin' at

71

their buckskins. One red as a damn full-blood, the other so fuckin' blond you'd think she'd just jumped off a Norski whaler!

"You could tell they were both half-wild." The grizzled mountain man leaned toward Longarm, widening his lake blue eye and making the eyeball dance as though electrified. "*Crazy looks in their eyes!*"

"Must be more than just crazy, since they're able to lure men in so they and their old man can kill 'em."

"Oh, yeah, they're more than just crazy," Comanche John hooted, watching Greta haul a large wooden tray out of the kitchen, steam wafting up from the four heaping plates. When she set the tray on the table, Comanche snaked his right hand under her left arm and squeezed her large left breast through her dress and apron. "They're both built like clipper ships!"

"Comanche *John*!" she exclaimed, wiggling away from him and raising her small, pudgy fist. "My beau vill feex you like thees!"

She shook her fist then removed two plates from the tray and set them gently before Longarm, her brown eyes meeting his with a soft, coquettish glow. One of the plates was entirely mounded with chopped potatoes fried with butter and sauerkraut, while the other bore four easy-over eggs and two eight-inch lengths of fat venison sausage fairly bursting its skin and reeking of black pepper.

As the mountain man chuckled at the girl's pluck, Greta set the other two plates before him, snorting and slamming them down huffily before sweeping a lock of stray hair from her cheek. "You very horny old dog!" she told John as she picked up her tray and set it on her shoulder. "I hope those crazy vimen in mountains pop you on head!"

Comanche John made smooching sounds and, picking up his silverware, winked at Longarm. As Greta disappeared back into the kitchen, John said, "The woman's crazy about me, mark me. Her beau knows it. Valentine

Fettig. Big son of a bitch of an ugly Prussian muleskinner. I don't stay in town long when he's around. One of the few white bastards who can whip me in a fair fight."

Longarm had thought that with the vast breakfast before them, Comanche John would hold his tongue for a bit and let Longarm eat in peace. It was, after all, still early.

But by the time they were scrubbing the last bit of yokes from their plates with chunks of venison sausage or potatoes, Longarm had a fair working knowledge of John's history—of the prime Irish stock from which he had descended, his own Indian war record as well as that of his father who'd fought in the war of 1812, and even that of his grandfather, the indomitable John Henry Blassingame, owner of lands and slaves in early New England.

"Don't worry, John," Longarm said, tossing down several coins then rising and plucking his half-smoked cigar from the table. "You got the job . . . if you'll do it for five dollars a day."

Longarm flicked his cigar to life on his thumbnail.

John clapped his hands loudly and laughed as he gained his feet. "I do tend to go on a bit. Five's right stingy for Uncle Sam, but I don't have nothin' else goin'. Say, you all outfitted, are ye?"

"I just have to pick up my horses at the Occidental. You?"

"I stabled mine with an old half-breed outta town aways. Why don't you go on ahead? I got a little business to tend here in town. I'll pick up my cayuses and meet you up trail in an hour or so."

"Sounds right as rain to me, John," Longarm said before turning and heading for the door, while puffing his cigar. He'd enjoy the hell out of that one quiet hour. It was bound to be a long trip up canyon with this blow-nasty uncle of Merle's. But if Comanche John knew the canyon as well as he claimed, he'd no doubt be worth a couple of sore eardrums.

"Uh . . . Longarm?"

The lawman turned with one hand on the doorknob. Comanche John stood on the other side of the table, adjusting his eye patch, his beard lifting with a buttery grin. "You reckon you could advance me . . . say . . . uh . . . one silver cartwheel? I got some notes comin' due."

Longarm tucked the cigar in the far right corner of his mouth to cover a wince. He plucked a gold eagle from his denims pocket and flipped it to Comanche John, whose meaty right paw snapped it out of the air like the practiced beak of a mud hen snatching a junebug in mid-flight.

"*Gracias, amigo!*" intoned Comanche John.

Longarm made a mental note to add the eagle to his expense sheet, then turned, went out, and set his hat for the Occidental Livery and Feed Barn.

Maybe the son of a bitch would prove more annoying than handy after all. But once you've fucked the niece, you're pretty much stuck with the uncle.

Chapter 8

Longarm was rigged up and moseying out of town, the pack mule following on a long lead rope, by the time the huge, liquid red sun had risen like a giant fire balloon out of the sage-pocked eastern prairie.

He'd started out wearing his sheepskin vest, as the nights and mornings were brisk most of the year at this altitude. But by the time he'd swung both horses along the low, cottonwood-stippled southern bank of the Diamondback River, the sun was branding his back and neck.

He stopped to roll the vest into his soogan and rain slicker. When he'd let both mounts draw water from a rocky ford, from which they'd scared up a good hundred barking and quarreling Canada geese, he mounted up and booted the muscular sorrel toward the mouth of Diamondback Canyon, a wedge-shaped gap in the sandstone and granite scarps rising in the west, at the base of higher, purple green peaks shouldering back against the far horizon.

Longarm was well within those high, crenelated walls pushing shade a good ways into the narrow canyon and over the frothy, tea-colored river, before he caught a glimpse of a rider galloping behind him—a big man in buckskins on a tall dun and trailing a black pack mule.

Longarm continued walking the sorrel along the rushing stream, following the deep-carved wagon trail through scattered aspens and cottonwoods, until the pounding of hooves rose above the river's rush.

He stopped the sorrel and looked behind.

Comanche John galloped toward him through the dappled shade of sprawling cottonwoods. He held his reins up high against his chest, the brim of his sombrero shading his face. The big man's buckskins were sweat-stained, and both his dun and the beefy mule were lathered and dusty.

"Hold up, John!" Longarm called, scowling. "No point in faggin' your animals. I'm not goin' anywhere."

Comanche John drew up abreast of Longarm, laughing. "I was afraid you might get lost." He snapped a quick look over his left shoulder. "Besides, old Roberta and Matthew been stabled too much of late, and need to get the juices flowin'." Again, he peered over his left shoulder to look behind with a cautious air, then turned back to Longarm. "We best get movin'. It's a good fifty miles to the pass."

He booted the dun mare forward, jerking the black mule along behind.

Longarm stared after the graybeard for a time, frowning, then hipped around in his saddle to peer back over the wagon trail cleaving the sun-splashed cottonwood copse. Spying only John's sifting dust and mountain jays and woodpeckers among the trees, he spurred the sorrel forward and caught up to John as the big man traced a long bend in the rocky-banked river.

"So tell me, Longarm," John said. "Are we huntin' ole Magnusson and those fiendish women of his, or are we hopin' they'll hunt us?"

"Both." Longarm poked his hat brim up to peer along the granite walls rising on both sides of the river. "You know where he'd hole up as well as anyone, don't you, John?"

"I know the canyon better'n most. And I know where his

cabins were as of three, four years ago. Since he went ape-crazy with killin', he might have abandoned those shacks and found him another. Hell, he could even be holed up in a cave. There's plenty up along the pass and around the base of Ute Peak."

Longarm winced as he peered around. You never fully realized the depth of a country until you rode into it—and this was a deep one, indeed.

"Maybe they'll come lookin' for us first, and save us the time and trouble of lookin' too long for *them*."

"Want I should pull my pecker out, Longarm?" Comanche John quipped, showing his entire set of ivory white teeth. "That'd git them girls down here right quick!"

John howled, scaring finches from a rocky, pine-stippled slope.

"Not just yet, John," Longarm said. "I'll tell you when."

They camped that night about fifteen miles up canyon, beyond the Diamondback Narrows, a gorge pinched down to only a few yards across, where the water spewed through the boulders and granite slabs like a geyser.

The night came early, the sun sinking down behind the unseen Skull Pass at the canyon's far end. Wolves howled. The stars were like crystals. There was so little breeze that Longarm, sitting on a low scarp near their bivouac, puffing his cheroot and sipping coffee, his Winchester across his knees, could hear the slightest scrape of two branches, the faint rustling of burrowing creatures, and the flaps of an owl sweeping invisibly over the canyon.

The river was a constant, distant murmur over nearby shallows.

When he returned to the bivouac, Comanche John sat on a log by the fire, reaching into a burlap bag sitting at his jackbooted feet. He pulled out a bottle wrapped in deerskin and knotted twine. His eyes were glassy as he ran a thick, knobby hand down the bottle before holding it out to the fire, staring at the deep amber glow within.

"I reckon I see where that gold piece went," Longarm said, walking over and prodding the sack with his boot toe. Another bottle rolled out of the bag's mouth, wrapped in deerskin.

"Now, see here, Deputy," Comanche John said, carefully shoving the bottle back into the sack. "You think I'm low enough to shake you down for ten dollars, then go off and spend it on *hooch*?" He gazed up at Longarm from beneath his shaggy, gray brows. "The uncle of Diamondback's noble *marshal*?"

"That's what I'm thinkin'."

John stared up at him, brows beetled, face flushing angrily, firelight dancing in his eyes. Finally, a sheepish grin broke over his weathered, bearded features. He popped the cork from the bottle in his hands. "Pshaw! I reckon you already spied the brand on this old reprobate!" He held the bottle up. "Drink?"

Longarm extended his cup. Comanche John splashed some whiskey into Longarm's coffee, then slid down off the log to rest his back against it, extending his buckskin-clad legs straight out toward the fire and crossing his jackboots at the ankles.

Longarm sat on a rock to John's left. He rested his elbows on his knees and stared into the fire, sipped the whiskey-laced coffee. It wasn't Maryland rye, but it wasn't bad.

After a few pensive minutes staring into the burning coals, wondering how many days it would take to run old Magnusson down, then remembering he'd forgotten to cable a report to Billy before leaving Diamondback, he turned to see John regarding him like the cat who ate the canary, his teeth as well as his eyes glistening like brands in the firelight.

"Fess up, Longarm," John said. "What was she like?"

Longarm frowned over his cup rim. "What was who like?"

"What was *who* like?" John mocked. "Why, Merle, of course! Are you tellin' me you didn't share her mattress sack? Pshaw! A man big and handsome as you? Merle keeps her knees clamped so tight you couldn't pry 'em apart with a crowbar, but"—he slitted his eyes—"I suspicion she might've opened 'em fer you."

Longarm plucked a cigar from his shirt pocket and bit off the end. "What a question for an uncle to ask of his niece."

"Shit, you seen her. Even an uncle can tell she's built like a brick shithouse. And, hell, I heared her damn screams last night all the way over to Old Louis's whorehouse on the bank of the Diamondback!" John slapped his thigh, thrust his chin at the stars, and guffawed.

As if to reply, coyotes yipped and yammered on a nearby ridge.

"John, a gentleman don't kiss and blabber . . . especially to the lady's uncle."

Chagrined, John furrowed his brows at him over the leaping flames.

"Now you tell *me* somethin'," Longarm said, tossing his hat down beside him and running a brusque hand through his hair. "Who the hell's trailin' us?"

John looked stunned. "Huh?"

"I spied their dust trail a couple hours ago. Three, four riders. Just before the sun went down, I saw a sun flash off either a rifle barrel or a field glass lens."

"Whiskey must be gettin' to you. Better lay off, Longarm." John took a pull.

Longarm stared at him. "You don't know anything about 'em?"

John scowled into the fire. "Sometimes the railroad sends market hunters out thisaway when the game's done been shot off the plains. Hell, they could be prospectors.

Been some good washings in this canyon of late . . . in spite of that kill-crazy trio workin' their evil deeds."

"I reckon you're right. They could be prospectors. They could also be dissatisfied creditors who spied you spending that gold eagle I gave you on whiskey instead of puttin' it toward, say, maybe, a grocery bill or a gambling debt."

Comanche John glared at him. "Longarm, you think I'm hock-high to a shithouse rat, don't ya?"

"Well, you did spend the gold eagle on hooch, and you are rather interested in your niece's bedroom habits . . ."

John corked his bottle and heaved himself to his feet, staggering a little and punching his open palm with the other fist. "Okay, goddamnit, Longarm. I just gotta know. I ain't gonna be satisfied till I'm clear on who's the tougher son of a bitch—you or me!"

Longarm stared up at the man from beneath his cinnamon brows. "Huh?"

John motioned for him to stand. "Come on. Git up!"

Longarm continued staring at him. John seemed to get crazier by the hour. Had Merle been pulling a practical joke, recommending the loco mossy-horn for a mountain guide?

The big graybeard kicked his empty coffee cup from the fire ring. "Come on, damnit." Wheeling, he began unbuttoning his right shirt cuff as he ambled over to a flat boulder on the far side of the bivouac, near where the horses and mules stood grazing idly at their hitch rope. Rolling the sleeve up his arm, he knelt on the far side of the rock and stared over the rock's flat, fissured surface at Longarm.

"Git up, now, damnit! Don't be yalla. I gotta know which one's tougher—you or me."

"Give the owls in your tree a rest, John," Longarm snorted, remaining on his own rock and tipping his coffee cup to his lips. "They're right tuckered, and so am I."

"Get over here, blast ya!" John was working on the other sleeve. "It's drivin' me crazy. I gotta know!"

Longarm looked over the fire at the crazy mountain man hunkered down on the far side of the boulder. John had both sleeves rolled up his long, pale, muscle-corded, knife-scarred arms, and he was carefully brushing sand and pine needles from atop the rock.

"You wanna arm wrestle," Longarm said, elbows on his knees, one brow arched as he scrutinized his crazy partner.

John laughed without mirth and set his right elbow atop the rock, flexing his hand. "You're right quick for a federal badge-toter!"

Longarm sat there for a time, feeling ridiculous. He looked around, half-expecting to spot Merle, watching from afar and snickering her pretty head off.

Finally, Longarm chuckled dryly. It was pretty plain the conversation about the men behind them was closed. He threw back the last of his coffee and whiskey and dropped the cup by the fire. He felt as though he'd slipped back about twenty-five years, and the playground bully was calling him out for the right to ask the freckle-faced girl to the barn dance.

"All right, John."

He stood and swept his hair back from his forehead, and, strolling over to Comanche John eyeing him like a hungry bobcat, he unbuttoned his right leather shirt cuff and rolled the sleeve up above his elbow.

"We playin' for nickles, dimes, quarters . . . ?"

"Braggin' rights," said the mountain man. "Come on. Git down here and put up your paw!"

Longarm pinched his trousers up his thighs and dropped to one knee. He planted his right elbow atop the rock, locking gazes with Comanche John, and moved his elbow around a little, getting comfortable.

Comanche John set his left hand up in front of his right elbow, palm open, as if to shake. Longarm did likewise, taking the old man's hand in his, feeling the dry, calloused fingers close around his own.

It was obvious right off the bat that John couldn't beat him. At least, not in his inebriated state. Longarm let their locked fists swing back and forth a few times, like the pendulum on a wound-down clock. After about a minute, however, he feigned exhaustion and let his arm go limp.

John slammed his knuckles into the boulder.

"Hawwwwwwwww! By jove, you slick little river rat, I won!"

There's your bragging rights, as if you needed them, Longarm thought.

"You're one tough son of a bitch, John." Longarm gained his feet. "Now, you mind if I get some shut-eye?"

"Know what you done wrong?" John said, grinning across the rock. "You done used up too much strength at the beginnin', tryin' to whup me right off! I seen it many a time in the overconfident. Ha!"

Longarm shook his head and headed back to the fire. "I'm gonna have to remember that."

John said behind him, "Another thing you might do, Longarm—if'n you wanna keep arm wrastlin', that is—is strengthen the muscles in your forearm. Guys like you, you're all shoulders. That's all right if you're just tossin' feed sacks to and fro, and if'n you're just out to bag pussy. But that ole forearm is important, too."

John stood, brushed sand and pinecones from his knees, and swaggered over to the fire, chin lifted like the prow of a clipper ship cleaving a smooth sea, his gaze proud as that of a young panther bringing fresh kill back to the cave.

"Yes, sir, I might be on the lee side of sixty, but I can still whup you pups. Maybe not every time. I ain't sayin' that. Don't call *me* cocky. But every now and then I'll surprise ye!"

Longarm took a long pull from his bottle of Maryland rye. His nerves were shot. The only thing more exhausting than a hard trail was a braggart. He kicked off his boots.

"I'm done wore out, John. I'm gonna call it a night. You mind keepin' the first watch?"

No doubt, the oldster's swollen head would keep him awake for a couple of hours anyway.

John laughed as Longarm crawled into his soogan and drew several blankets up to his chest.

"Ah, hell, I don't mind. You city boys need your sleep. I'll wake ye in a couple hours." John prodded Longarm's right calf with the toe of his jackboot. "Say, Longarm?"

Longarm looked up at the graybeard towering over him.

"Just be glad we weren't fightin' with our bare-knuckled fists." He winked, then picked up his old Spencer repeater and blustered off into the darkness.

Longarm lay his head on his saddle and tipped his hat brim low. "Mercy."

Chapter 9

The Mexican said, "They are stopped on the trail, right side of the river. Comanche John is pointin' at something on the ground."

"Maybe he finally found his marbles," said Crazy Eddie Lancer, chuckling as he raised a whiskey bottle to his thin lips.

"Shut up and cork the bottle, Eduardo," ordered Natcho as he continued staring through the spyglass.

It was mid-afternoon of the next day, and the man known only as Natcho swept a greasy tangle of black hair from his forehead as he snugged the spyglass to his right eye, scrutinizing the two men—Comanche John and his unknown, dark-haired partner—whom Natcho and his two companions had been following for the past two days.

"What're they lookin' at, Natcho?" asked Wilbur Keats, sitting with Crazy Eddie in the rocks beneath Natcho.

Keats and Crazy Eddie Lancer were sitting with their backs to the black-granite scarp, passing a whiskey bottle and smoking hastily rolled quirleys. The cigarette smoke wafted up to Natcho, as did the pungent odor of the cheap strychnine whiskey the men had bought at a roadhouse outside Casper two days ago.

In the spyglass's sphere of magnification, Comanche John rose up from his haunches and waved an arm around, indicating directions. Comanche John's partner booted the sorrel straight up trail. Comanche John heaved himself into his own saddle, then reined his dun down the riverbank. He rode through a row of aspens, across the small rocks lining the shore, and into the water.

The hooves of the horse and the mule sent up a fine, white spray sparkling in the sunlight.

"What's goin' on?" asked Wilbur Keats.

Natcho slid the spyglass back right. Comanche John's partner was trotting his sorrel and pack horse up a low rise, the handles of the picks and shovels tucked into the panniers nodding with the pack horse's movements.

When the man had disappeared down the other side of the rise, Natcho slid the spyglass left again. Comanche John had mounted the river's opposite bank. He appeared to be heading for the mouth of an off-shooting ravine.

Natcho lowered the spyglass, reduced it, and stuck it into the fringed sheath hanging around his neck. "They split up," he said as he leaped off the scarp, landing on the lower ledge between Crazy Eddie and Wilbur Keats. He continued on down the shelf toward their horses tethered in the ravine.

"Split up?" said Keats, the biggest of the three, breathing hard as he followed Natcho and Crazy Eddie.

"John is headin' into a ravine, south side of the river. Nearest I can figure, they are looking for a claim." Natcho leaped the slope's last few feet and landed flat-footed in a patch of bromegrass. To his left, the three horses tied to spindly cedar shrubs eyed the men expectantly, the high-altitude sun dancing on Natcho's silver-mounted black saddle and bridle chains.

"What if he don't have the money on him?" Keats asked as Natcho turned his left stirrup out, then swung into the leather.

Natcho put his black-and-white pinto toward the canyon, whipping the horse's left hip with his rein ends and digging his spurs into the mount's flanks. "We take it out of his hide."

He was halfway across the river when the other two caught up to him, one on either side, shod hooves ringing off the half-submerged rocks. As they gained the river's low, southern bank, Natcho shucked his brass-breeched Henry repeater from its scabbard, cocked it one-handed, and turned the pinto toward the ravine mouth, glancing down to see John's tracks gouged in the sparse weeds and river sand.

Pressing a finger to his mustachioed lips for quiet, and grinning evily, he turned to the others, who fell in behind him, walking their horses single-file as they cleaved the ravine's mouth.

Being mere drifters and occasional drovers, Crazy Eddie and Wilbur Keats deferred to Natcho, who'd been a Texas shootist and border bandit before running north from Mexican bounty hunters.

The three followed a narrow trail along a seep, into the ravine's soft purple shadows. About fifty yards in, the ravine's rocky, brush-tufted walls fell back, and woods opened on the left and across the seep on the right.

Bird and squirrels chittered. Springs murmured up from mossy stones.

They'd passed several dry sluice traps and the remains of an old mining shack, when Natcho drew rein and raised his rifle for the others to follow suit. About forty yards ahead, where the trail began a slow swing toward the right along an aspen copse, a black mule's ass protruded from the woods, tail swishing lazily. Natcho could make out part of a dirty canvas pack saddle.

He waved to Crazy Eddie and Wilbur Keats, then reined his horse hard left, and in seconds they were dismounting behind a low knoll among cedars and buffalo grass. No one said a word as they tied their mounts to the spindly shrubs. Then, Keats and Crazy Eddie following Natcho while holding their old-model repeaters up high across their chests, they crept toward the half-concealed pack mule.

Natcho stopped and turned to the others. He kept his voice low. "I will circle around. Keep going and, for the love of Mary, don't make any noise!"

Wilbur Keats wrinkled his nose indignantly as Natcho slipped into the trees on the right side of the trail, moving soundlessly on his low-heeled, black boots.

"Fuckin' bean-eater thinks we're a coupla moon-calves," he groused and continued tramping up trail, Crazy Eddie on his left.

"I'd have back-shot him a long time ago if he wasn't so good at gettin' us women," Crazy Eddie whispered.

"Shhh," Keats said as they approached a broad birch, moving up to within twenty yards of the black pack mule beyond the tree.

They were ten feet from the birch, quartering around its left side, when a large figure suddenly stepped out from behind it. Comanche John held a long-barreled Colt Navy in one hand and a broad-bladed Bowie knife in the other. The horsehair thong of his sugarloaf sombrero hung loose beneath his chin.

He grinned from ear to ear, white teeth flashing in his slate gray beard.

"If you fuckin' dunderheads think you can sneak up on Comanche John, you got another *think* comin'!"

There was a wooden thud, and John's head jerked forward. He closed his eye and pinched up his cheeks as he stumbled toward Keats and Crazy Eddie, dropping first his pistol and then his knife before falling to his knees with a grunt.

Slumping forward on his hands, he shook his head and snorted like an enraged bull buffalo with arrows in its flanks.

Natcho stepped up behind John, lowering the butt of his Henry, a foxy grin lifting the corners of his knife-slash mouth, framed by long, drooping mustaches. "If you say so, Jose!"

Longarm's sorrel and pack mule splashed through the sun-dappled river specked with old leaves and occasional branches, and mounted the opposite bank.

Longarm swept the ground with his gaze, looking for more wolf sign like that which Comanche John had spotted on the other side of the river, among three sets of unshod horse tracks. Being a primitive, without regular access to a blacksmith's forge, Magnusson probably let his horses go barefoot . . .

The lawman drew rein as his eyes scanned the moist sand pocked with several sets of horse tracks—these all shod.

Five, by his count. All five sets looked fresh.

It looked as though John was leading a parade up the ravine yonder.

Longarm shucked his Winchester from the saddle boot and heeled the sorrel ahead. At the ravine's mouth, he tied the pack mule in high grass and shrubs, then remounted the sorrel and headed up the ravine, following the tracks etching the muddy trail before him.

Ten minutes later, angry voices rose on the breeze, above the tinny murmur of the freshet on his right. The smacks of thrown punches sounded, with anguished grunts and groans.

Longarm slipped out of his saddle, dropped the sorrel's reins, and jogged ahead, staying as far left as he could, peering around a slow, right bend in the trail. When he spied movement about forty yards away, at the edge of the aspen copse, he dodged behind a high knoll stippled with occasional cedars and boulders, and climbed the knoll's backside.

The voices grew louder as he gained the top of the knoll and started down the other side, weaving through small scarps and a few stunt pines. He stopped about halfway down the knoll, between a craggy thumb of rust-colored sandstone and a lone pine.

In the clearing before him, between the trail and the aspens, Comanche John stood in a loose circle formed by three men in dusty trail clothes, circling John like wolves on the death scent. Bloody-faced and hatless, John held his fists high as he bobbed and weaved and spat curses, berating and baiting his attackers, coaxing them on.

One of the men—big and fleshy and wearing a shabby opera hat with a red silk band—was on his knees, cursing and crossing his hands over his crotch. John swung toward a short, wiry gent with blood trickling down his busted lip, a battered, funnel-brimmed Stetson lying nearby.

"You fuckin', old, cheatin' bastard!" the wiry gent shouted, then swung his right fist at John's head.

Comanche John parried the blow, the wiry gent's fist glancing off John's forearm. John stepped forward with surprising grace for a man his age and size, and jabbed his left into the wiry gent's face with a solid smack.

"*Unnghhh!*" the wiry gent cried as blood from his smashed nose sprayed across his face.

As the wiry gent staggered back, clutching his ruined nose, the third man—a Mexican in bull-hide chaps and a black vest adorned with small, silver conchos—strode smoothly toward John, grinning. As John turned toward him, the Mexican laid two quick jabs, one with each fist, against John's cheeks.

Then he buried his right fist into John's gut.

When John leaned forward with a massive grunt, spewing air from his lungs, the Mexican rammed his right knee into John's face.

Howling like a moon-crazed lobo, the Mexican turned and danced away from John.

Wheeling back toward his quarry with a mocking flourish, the Mexican drew his Colt from the cross-draw holster on his left hip, thumbing back the hammer as he closed his fingers around the hide-wrapped grips.

On the side of the knoll, Longarm loudly jacked a shell into the Winchester's breech and aimed the rifle straight out from his right hip.

"Fandango's over, friends!"

The Mexican whipped his head toward him. So did the fat man still down on his knees and the wiry gent now holding only one hand to his nose while the other hand fingered the grips of his holstered six-shooter.

The three stood frozen, glaring at Longarm. Comanche John turned toward the lawman, as well, blinking blood from his eye, half-lowering his fists.

Holding his revolver about four inches above his holster, the Mexican shaped another grin, his black eyes cunning. "Mister, I'm betting you cannot fire accurately from that distance and position."

Longarm squeezed the Winchester's trigger.

"*Ahhhh!*" the Mexican cried as the bullet drilled the revolver in his hand. The gun dropped several feet behind him, the force of the shot spinning him toward the trees and dropping him to his knees.

Clutching his bloody right hand in his left, he turned his slit-eyed, hard-jawed glance over his right shoulder. "Son of a *bitch!*"

Longarm raked his gaze across the other two men, saw the hefty gent sliding his pudgy, gloved right hand toward his own six-shooter while staring at Longarm. Longarm swung the Winchester toward him, and blew the opera hat off his head.

The man screamed and ducked as his hat, a ragged hole in the red silk band, rolled off on the breeze.

"Anyone else?" Longarm asked, swinging the Winchester from left to right and back again.

Comanche John lowered his fists to his sides and chuckled.

The skinny gent with the broken nose yelled as though from the bottom of a deep well, blood spraying from his smashed nostrils with every breath. "That old bastard done fleeced us at cards in Valentine. Won five hundred dollars off'n us with a marked deck!"

Longarm glanced at John, who pointed at the skinny gent and lifted his chin toward Longarm. "I done told 'em I'd pay 'em back when I got to Diamondback. But no, they wanted it right then and there on the trail. Well, goddamnit, boys, I don't have it." He leaned back on his heels and threw his head back, guffawing. "And I reckon you found out what happens when you try takin' it out of my hide."

"Shut up, John," Longarm said.

Comanche John closed his mouth and scowled, brushing blood from his eye with the back of his hand.

Longarm looked at the men who'd been trailing them. "You three, toss down your weapons and get the hell outta here. I see you again, I won't be near this friendly."

The Mexican was wrapping his neckerchief around his hand, scowling up at Longarm. "What about our money?"

"You'll have to take that up with John . . . when I'm out of the picture. As long as I'm in it, I'll perforate your hides if you come after him again." Longarm jerked the Winchester barrel down ravine. "Now, break a leg."

When the men had tossed down their weapons and slouched off indignantly, the skinny gent shoving bits of his torn neckerchief up his nose, the Mexican cursing and clutching his wounded hand, the beefy gent walking bull-legged and donning his bullet-torn opera hat, Longarm descended the knoll.

Comanche John stood in the middle of the clearing, smiling at Longarm, blinking blood from his eye. Longarm approached the man, scowling, raising his Winchester straight out from his waist.

John backed away, lifting his hands to his shoulders, palms out. "Now, wait a minute, Longarm. Don't do nothin' hasty! I'm the one that spied that wolf scat! You'd have ridden right on by!"

Longarm snugged the Winchester's barrel against John's belly. John tensed, balling his gray-furred cheeks and slitting his eye, awaiting the shot. Longarm wasn't about to shoot him, but for several seconds he enjoyed the fantasy.

He removed the barrel from the mountain man's belly and depressed the hammer. "You find any sign up this way?"

Comanche John swallowed, his sheepish grin returning, and lowered his hands. He shook his head. "Not even a track."

"I found more wolf prints just ahead of the shit pile across the river. Horse tracks, too." Longarm turned and began walking down ravine, resting his rifle barrel on his shoulder. "Come on."

"Can't I take a moment to tend myself?" John said behind him, voice hoarse with indignation. "In case you can't see, Longarm, I'm a bit disheveled!"

"You can tend yourself tonight. I wanna stay on that wolf's trail while it's fresh."

Chapter 10

When Natcho, Keats, and Crazy Eddie had retrieved their horses, they splashed back across the river in moody silence. When they'd gained the main trail hugging the canyon's north wall, Natcho drew rein. Hunkered over his wounded hand, he gazed west, his eyes pain-wracked and fury-glazed.

He'd replaced his lost Colt in his holster with a spare from his saddlebags, as had Crazy Eddie. Wilbur Keats didn't have a spare six-shooter, but he still had his saddle gun—a Spencer .56.

"Where the hell we goin', Natcho?" said Crazy Eddie, bits of bloody neckerchief hanging from his swollen nose. Already, his eyes were turning purple. "We ain't gonna turn tail on that son of a bitch, are we?"

"Listen, boys," Wilbur Keats grunted, shifting uncomfortably in his saddle to make room for his swollen balls. "I don't know about you, but I'm ready to write off my share of that five hundred dollar fleecin'. Comanche John's partner"—the lumpy man shook his head grimly—"no thanks!"

"Shut up, coward," grated Natcho through gritted teeth

as he hipped around in his saddle to look back across the river.

"Come on, Natcho," Keats said, wincing, his chubby, patch-bearded cheeks streaked with sweat and grime, "I think I might have some permanent damage. I'd like for a sawbones to check me out."

Crazy Eddie laughed nasally and punched Keats in the arm. "Ah, what're you worried about, Wilbur? You never had any balls in the first place!"

Natcho booted his horse westward. "Fall in, amigos. An old Ute woman works at the roadhouse up yonder. Uglier than Diablo's bride, but she knows some healin'."

"Ah, Christ," grunted Keats, hunkered over his saddle horn. "I'd just as soon have a *white man* inspect my oysters."

Crazy Eddie laughed again. "What—you think the ole dog-eater's gonna cut 'em *off*?" He sobered as his horse followed Natcho's high-stepping pinto. "I tell you what I want. I want another run at ole Comanche John and his friend that's so handy with that long gun. I'm gonna take that Winchester of his, shove it up his ass, and pull the fucking trigger . . ."

"You'll get your chance," Natcho said without turning around.

An hour later, as the sun angled behind the toothy western ridges, they drew up before a roadhouse nestled in a little gap in the rocky, cedar-stippled bluffs on the north side of the trail.

"Ah, *fuck*!" Crazy Eddie complained as he ran his gaze over the hovel, its tin chimney pipe smokeless, the windows shuttered, a padlock on the door. There were no sounds from inside, no horses in the corral or lean-to stable flanking the shack's right side. "No one's here!"

Wilbur Keats leaned out from his saddle, studying the sheet of moisture-stained paper fluttering from a nail in the right door casing. He moved his lips, trying to sound out the words.

Natcho turned to Crazy Eddie, the only one of the three who could read. "What's it say, Professc ?"

Crazy Eddie leaned out from his own saddle, slitting his eyes. Haltingly, he recited the words penciled on the breeze-jostled leaf.

"Closed . . . till crazy mountain man and his wolf girls . . . are hung."

Natcho cursed.

Crazy Eddie looked at him. "What crazy mountain man?"

"I never heard nothin' about it," said Keats. "Ain't been through this country in a time."

"Crazy mountain man?" Natcho chuffed. "You ever known one that *ain't* crazy?"

He frowned suddenly, lifting his chin and squinting his eyes. He'd heard something.

A woman's laugh?

"What the hell was that?" said Crazy Eddie.

It came again, like a chime wafting on the wind. It was a woman's laugh. No doubt about it.

Natcho hipped around in his saddle, trying to follow the sound to its source. It had come from the river. He stared at the scattered pines and aspens impeding his view of the Diamondback, the wind ruffling the leaves.

Female voices rose. A giggle.

Suddenly, a horse's head pushed through a low-hanging aspen branch. The horse mounted the bank, the branch swiping over it, two riders ducking beneath the rustling leaves.

The horse's hooves clomped and rang off stones. When the mount had cleared the tree, the two young women on its blanketed back lifted their heads, giggling.

"I'll . . . be . . . damned," muttered Keats.

Natcho blinked as the women pulled the brown-and-white paint onto the trail and reined it up canyon—two young women, probably in their early twenties, one with light features and curly, golden hair, the other with the dusky red features and the coal black hair of a full-blooded Indian. The Indian girl sat in front of the blonde, holding the braided rawhide reins up high against her full breasts pushing at the low-cut deerskin dress.

Three large, gutted jackrabbits hung down from the saddlehorn before her—the fur bloody, eyes open.

The dark-haired girl turned toward Natcho and the others and halted the horse. The blonde followed her gaze, lips stretching back from her teeth in a grin.

The dark-haired girl smiled smokily, keeping her lips pressed together. She clucked the horse forward, continuing up canyon, hers and the blonde's rich hair jostling down their backs.

"Are my balls so sore I'm hallucinatin'?" asked Wilbur Keats.

"If you're seein' a couple purty women on a paint horse," said Crazy Eddie, "then I reckon we're *both* hallucinatin'."

"You boys wait here," Natcho said, reining his pinto after the girls. "Neither one of you is in any condition for romance."

"Shit, you're sayin' your hand don't hurt?" Crazy Eddie chuffed.

"A wounded hand doesn't put a Mexican out of the mood for love, Eduardo."

"Wait up, Natcho," Wilbur called. "I think my oysters are beginnin' to regain their natural size and color."

"My nose just started feelin' better, too," said Eddie, booting his white-socked dun after Natcho.

When the Mexican was about ten yards behind the girls trotting their paint up canyon under a canopy of darkening aspen leaves, the blonde looked back, grinning.

"Whoa, there, señoritas!"

The dark-haired girl turned toward him coolly while the blonde continued smiling at him over her right shoulder. The girl holding the reins checked the horse down and neck-reined it toward Natcho. The Mexican reined his own horse to a halt and poked his hat back off his forehead as he ran his eyes over the two incredible creatures before him, a hard ball forming in his throat.

Both were clothed in what looked like deerskin rags—if you could call it clothed. One strap of the blonde's dress hung down to her right elbow, revealing all but the nipple of a hard, round breast, golden from where the sun had tanned it. Her dress was edged with rabbit furs and trimmed with talismans in the form of bear teeth and died porcupine quils and racoon claws shaped like the sun and moon.

The dark-haired girl's dress was similar but simpler, and instead of talismans adorning it, she wore a necklace of white trade beads and bear teeth around her long, regal, adobe-colored neck.

While the blonde's hair hung around her head in deliciously messy curls streaked with trail dust and seeds, the dark girl's coal black hair hung straight down her back, glistening with bear tallow and trimmed with a faint spray of Indian paintbrush. Her breasts, too, were full and round, the low-cut dress exposing the deep cleft between.

The girls' legs were exposed from their knees down, the long calves muscular and smooth. Both were barefoot, their feet dusty.

He smelled a gamey musk emanating from them both.

The blonde, her blue eyes sparkling, stared at him while speaking to the girl in front of her. "He has a question for us!"

Natcho had been about to ask them about the Ute healing woman, but their beauty was like a direct blow from an axe handle. He chuckled as the other two men rode up behind him, their horses blowing, their silence revealing how deep down their throats their tongues had slipped, awestruck by the girls' beauty.

"Yes, ma'am," Natcho said, removing his hat with a

flourish then holding it across his heart, "I was just wondering to what blessing of fate do my *compañeros* and I owe the honor of sharing the same trail as such a beautiful pair of señoritas."

"What's he jawin' about, Raven?" asked the blonde, wrinkling the bridge of her nose as she stared at Natcho. "I didn't understand a *word.*"

"I think we have been complimented, Sunflower." For the first time, the dark-haired girl called Raven smiled, her perfectly sculpted cheeks dimpling. "I think we are being what the white-eyes call *courted.*"

"Courted?" Sunflower laughed throatily. "Does that mean they want to *fuck* us?"

Natcho's face warmed. The blonde laughed again, harsher than before. Raven's smile grew, her almond-shaped, black eyes slitting alluringly.

"Christalmighty!" whooped Crazy Eddie, his smashed nose making it sound more like a bull elk's raspy bugle. "Sunflower and *Raven!*"

"Only if the, uh . . . fucking so delights you, of course," Natcho said, bowing his head slightly at the women, the corners of his mouth drawing up.

Sunflower giggled. It was the same giggle they'd heard through the trees.

Raven shunted her dark gaze around the three men before her. "If you are looking for the healer, she and her man pulled foot a month ago."

"Afraid of the . . . what was it?" Natcho glanced at the abandoned cabin behind him. "Wolf women?"

"*Sí,*" said Raven, eyes sparkling with pride in her Spanish.

"And the crazy mountain man they run with," said Sunflower, leaning forward and speaking in a loud whisper, as if sharing a secret. "Pure-dee kill-crazy, we hear." She winked.

"Ugly creatures, too, I bet," said Wilbur Keats, finally finding his tongue. "Prob'ly an old prospector's tale!"

"Of course," said Raven. She returned her gaze to Natcho. "Follow us, if you wish, and we'll tend your wounds."

She threw her hair back and gigged the paint forward. "It just so happens we are spending the evening alone." She flashed a devilish smile over her right shoulder. "And we are lonely!"

Both girls laughed like witches . . . beautiful, beguiling witches.

Natcho stared after them, heart pounding, his loins heavy. He glanced at the two men behind him. Both Crazy Eddie and Wilbur Keats looked as though they'd been struck by lightning as they stared after the girls.

"What the fuck are we waiting for, amigos?"

Natcho ground his spurs into the pinto's flanks.

The girls set a harried pace as they rode up canyon a good mile then turned right off the trail and headed into a broad, off-shooting ravine.

Several times Natcho lost sight of them as they galloped through rolling, broken country. They were even harder to keep pace with once the sun went down.

Natcho stopped his horse a couple of times to listen for their hoofbeats.

He wasn't sure where in the hell they were. Wariness was beginning to prick at him, when a pale, triangular object came into view about thirty yards ahead, at the base of a high, rock wall, just beyond a starlit, murmuring stream. The two girls and the paint horse were swaying and dodging silhouettes in front of it.

A teepee, Natcho saw as he crossed the stream and drew rein before the girls' blowing horse. There was a large fire ring before the teepee. From a high, stout branch of a nearby cottonwood, a large, hide-wrapped bundle hung fifteen feet off the ground. Probably a grub cache out of the reach of coons and bears.

Natcho kept his hand on his revolver's grips as he looked around, Crazy Eddie and Wilbur Keats reining up on either side of him, men and horses breathing hard from the cross-country run through the darkness.

"I thought for sure my horse was gonna break a leg!" Keats said, wiping sweat from his face.

"I ain't so sure about this," said Crazy Eddie. He, too, had his hand on his pistol. "How do we know these two ain't . . ." He let his voice trail off as he looked around the bivouac and the creek.

"Wolf women?" said Natcho, teeth showing against his dark face in the darkness. "Do they look like wolves to you?"

Raven walked toward them as Sunflower began leading the paint into the trees left of the teepee. Raven threw an arm out to indicate a pile of wood beside the fire ring. "You men build a fire. Sunflower and I will provide food and medicine. You may spread your bedrolls out around the fire. You can stay here this evening."

"You can stay *here* this evening!" laughed Sunflower as she and the horse disappeared in the darkness. "Build a big fire," she called above the sound of crunching weeds and branches. "I like *big fires*!"

"No menfolk about?" Crazy Eddie asked from atop his dun.

"Our . . . men are up canyon," said Raven, turning and striding toward the teepee.

"Prospectors or hunters?" asked Natcho. It was damn odd for men to leave women—especially a pair as beautiful as these—alone out here. But maybe that's why they left them in such an isolated place. Besides, in spite of their obvious femininity, these two looked capable of taking care of themselves.

"What do you think, Natcho?" said Keats, sitting his saddle to Natcho's left.

Natcho remembered the womanly curves he'd spied beneath the torn, dirty dresses, the full breasts fairly spilling from the deer hide. They'd smelled like something wild.

Blood pounded in his loins.

His ears rang at the prospect of sharing a bedroll with either one.

"Stake the horses, Wilbur," he said as he swung down from the saddle. "Me and Eddie will get started on that *big* fire!"

Chapter 11

While Crazy Eddie stripped and staked the horses by the creek, Natcho and Wilbur Keats built a fire large enough to roast a sow.

Meanwhile, Sunflower went to work skinning the field-dressed rabbits with the quick assuredness of a practiced hunter, her breasts swinging back and forth behind her dress as she worked, grunting and slicing with her skinning knife.

She didn't seem to mind the blood splashing her torn, smoke-stained dress and her hair. Her neck and the top third of her tits glistened gold in the firelight, offering Natcho and Keats a balm for their cuts and bruises as they spread out their saddles and blanket rolls a short distance from the crackling flames.

The nights got cold at this altitude, even in summer, but the large fire precluded the need for coats.

Crazy Eddie walked over from the creek, and Natcho broke out a fresh whiskey bottle. They passed around the bottle while Sunflower spitted the rabbits and Raven, who'd been rustling around inside the teepee, stepped out and moved toward Natcho.

The black-haired girl had thrown a gray fox skin around

her shoulders. In one hand she carried a bowl reeking like kerosene, juniper, rose hips, and something else that could only be horse piss. In her other hand she carried a wad of burlap.

"Here comes Doctor Raven!" giggled Sunflower as she poked the last spit through the last quartered rabbit and set it far enough out from the fire that the meat would cook without charring.

Raven knelt beside Natcho. He smiled up at her, staring at her black eyes glistening with firelight as she dipped one of the burlap strips into the lumpy goo in the bowl. She removed the neckerchief from around Natcho's hand, tossed it into the fire, then lowered her head to inspect the hand closely.

Having her this close to him, touching him, gave him an instant hard-on.

The bullet hadn't broken any bones, but it had torn out a good bit of flesh between Natcho's right index finger and thumb. Since he was mildly intoxicated by the women and the whiskey, it looked worse than it felt.

"Not so bad," Raven said.

As she wrapped the poultice around his hand, Natcho stared at her breasts framed in ragged fox skin. They jounced as she worked. When she'd tied the burlap tightly around the wound, she gazed down at him, her eyes straying to his bulging crotch.

The corners of her mouth rising slightly, she raised his hand to her left breast. With his index finger, she traced a circle around the nipple pushing at the deerskin dress from behind. It felt like a small thimble at the end of the swollen globe.

"Does that feel better?" she asked huskily, her hair hanging down both sides of her regal face.

Natcho chuckled. He stretched out his fingers to engulf the entire breast in his hand. She rose slowly, the breast rising beyond his reach, her gaze holding his until she turned and moved to the other side of the fire, where Eddie reclined against his saddle.

Natcho's jaws tightened. He glanced to his left, where Wilbur Keats sat on a log, elbows on his knees, regarding Natcho with a mocking grin. Natcho cursed under his breath.

Sunflower was dancing between the teepee and the fire, trying to catch glowing cinders in her hands as though they were snowflakes, her short skirt leaping about her long, bare legs, curly blond hair dancing on her shoulders. Her body seemed to move in several directions at once.

On the other side of the fire, Raven knelt beside Crazy Eddie, who'd been watching Sunflower, awe-struck, his blue black nose and swollen eyes resembling the exaggerated cutout features in a Halloween pumpkin.

Now he turned to Raven. Eddie was holding the whiskey bottle. She pointed at it.

"Take a big drink," she said, spreading her hands to indicate "big."

He stared up at her, lower jaw still hanging, eyes puzzled.

"I'm going to set your nose," Raven explained.

Crazy Eddie smiled, a ghoulish expression on his battered face. "I think it's just cracked. It'll heal just fine. I done broke it before."

Raven took the bottle from Eddie's hand and lifted it to her own lips. She took a couple of long swallows, throwing her head far back on her shoulders. As she lowered the bottle, her lips made a hollow smack as they left the glass. She ran her hand across her mouth and thrust the bottle back at Eddie.

"Take a drink."

Eddie hesitated. He lifted the bottle slowly, took a pull. When he lowered it, his battered eyes looked skeptical.

Raven moved toward him, planted her left knee on his chest.

"Hey, hey . . . wait, now—!"

She pinched his swollen nose between her thumb and index finger, and gave it a little twist. Even across the fire, Natcho could hear the sinewy crunch.

"*Ohhh!*" Eddie screamed, clapping both hands to his nose as blood streamed from the bits of cloth hanging from his nostrils.

"There," Raven laughed, tossing several strips of the burlap over Eddie's head. "All better now."

Natcho laughed as Eddie bunched the burlap over his nose.

Raven stood and moved around the fire toward Keats, the bowl in her hand.

Natcho laughed. "Your turn, amigo. Show her where it hurts!"

Sunflower had stopped chasing cinders to squat in the grass between the teepee and the fire, knees together, elbows on her knees, cheeks in her hands. She appeared bemused by her sister's ministrations. She kneaded the grass with her bare toes.

Raven stopped before Keats. He looked up at her sheepishly. His face was red, brows beetled.

Natcho guffawed. Even Eddie, still holding his nose with the burlap, tittered behind the wrap.

"Ow!" Sunflower exclaimed. "Ow-eee!"

Keats grabbed the bowl out of Raven's hand, cast an angry look at Eddie and Natcho, then stepped over the log he'd been sitting on, and stomped off in the darkness.

On the other side of the fire, Sunflower howled and rubbed her crotch. Raven chuckled, grabbed the bottle away from Eddie, then squatted down beside her sister. She took a long pull from the bottle, then handed it to Sunflower, who took a couple of long pulls before corking it and tossing it to Natcho.

The Mexican, surprised by the girl's stength, caught the bottle above his head. Both women looked at him, laughing.

He laughed, then, too, removing the bottle's cork and taking a long pull. He had a good mind to go over and take one of the women by force, but something told him they'd be more fun if they were willing.

They all lounged around the fire, smoking and drinking and chuckling. Laughter broke out when Keats strode out of the darkness, looking just as sheepish as before but walking a little less bow-legged.

He set the poultice bowl down beside Raven with a cordial nod. Drawing his breeches away from his crotch, he gave both Natcho and Eddie an owly look, wrinkling his nostrils, then grabbed the bottle out of Eddie's hands and returned to his log.

They passed the bottle around the fire once more, then Sunflower, who'd been turning the meat and arranging the sticks around the flames, deemed it done. She tossed a rabbit quarter to each man, then gave one to her sister and plunked down in the dust and grass beside Raven again, legs bent before her so that they framed a diamond between them. She went to work on the sizzling meat in her fingers with the passion of a famished gandy dancer.

As he ate hungrily, hot grease dripping down his chin, Natcho looked at the girls' bare legs, over which the dancing firelight flickered. As his hunger abated, his lust grew.

He snapped the bones and sucked out the marrow, then tossed the bones into the fire. Standing, he wiped his hands on his breeches, then went over to Raven and wrapped his right hand around her arm.

"I've had enough of your teasing, señorita." He pulled her brusquely to her feet. She gave a clipped, half-surprised, half-delighted cry and dropped the rabbit carcass she'd been holding in her greasy hands.

Natcho drew her toward him, and to his surprise, he didn't have to force her. She threw her arms around his neck and kissed him hungrily, savagely, ramming her tongue into his mouth and grinding her crotch against his.

Behind her, Sunflower laughed and clapped her hands excitedly.

Raven suddenly pulled away from Natcho, giving his lip a final, painful bite, then turned away and, laughing, ran to the teepee and threw back the flap. She looked at Natcho. He walked to her heavy-footed, his shaft so hard that it pushed painfully against his trousers, his loins fairly exploding with desire.

"No fire sticks," Raven said, glancing at the Colt hanging off Natcho's thigh.

Natcho didn't give a shit. His eyes were on her heaving breasts, the cleavage glistening with perspiration, his mind roaming ahead to what she'd feel like pinned beneath him.

In seconds, he'd unbuckled the belt and let the pistol and holster fall. She grabbed his hand and pulled him into the teepee, which smelled like strange herbs and tobacco and musty hides. Several candles burned and dripped wax on a low shelf, offering meager light.

Raven scrambled over the bear hides and buffalo robes spread across the floor, and knelt before the row of candles. She crossed her arms before her supple body and lifted the dress up to her waist, revealing every inch of her slender legs and hips.

Pausing to adjust her grip, she raised her crossed elbows, and Natcho watched the deer-hide garment slide up her long, dusky body, jostling the dark-tipped breasts before passing over her face and climbing over her head, catching at her black hair as she cast the garment aside with a soft, windy rustle.

Raven's hair fell back into place. Her full breasts jutted. She laughed and stared at Natcho, who wasted no time undressing, albeit awkwardly, grunting as he stumbled around the lodge.

The girl ran her greasy hands over her breasts slowly, sighing as she cupped them, kneading the grease into them, the nipples hardening. Then she squatted, rubbed the grease into her crotch. Natcho was ripping off his balbriggans as Raven ran her hands down her belly to her crotch, black eyes glistening like obsidian in the candles' glow.

Her gaze smoldered like that of a half-wild animal with the springtime craze. Natcho's heart pounded in his temples, made his ears ring.

Finally, he knelt beside her, took her shoulders in his hands, pulled her toward him, and closed his mouth over hers. He threw her back on the robes. She spread her legs for him, grunting and cursing, running her hands down his back, the fingernails digging painfully into his skin. She raised her knees high and wide.

"Come on, you greaser bastard," she grunted. "Give it to me, you son of a bitch!"

Her voice was a vague rustle in Natcho's ringing ears as he rose up on his outstretched arms and ushered his throbbing shaft through her furred portal. The rabbit grease made for easy going, and he slid into her quickly, plundering her core.

"*Ohhhhh!*" she screamed, digging her nails into his shoulder blades and throwing her head back against the robes, mouth drawn wide.

"*Uhhnhhh!*" he cried, pain mixing with passion.

He thrust into her, and she ground her heels into his buttocks.

Only a few thrusts later, his loins exploded. Holding himself deep inside her, he lifted his chin toward the teepee's smoke hole glimmering with starlight.

"*Madre Maria!*"

His body convusled, his hips spasming, seed jetting into her.

He slumped atop her and, when he found his strength, rolled onto his back, one leg crossing hers. He was breathing hard, his skin slick with perspiration.

She lay on her back, running her hands through her hair, sweat-slick breasts glistening in the candlelight. With a laugh, she turned over and pressed her breasts to his chest, pinching his ears in her hands, jostling his head. "Don't think I'm going to let you fall asleep, hombre. We've just gotten started!"

She cackled wickedly and kissed him hard.

Later, after they'd coupled two more times and the candles were nearly out, she rolled away from him. Her breaths grew long and slow.

"*Gracias, Jesus,*" he muttered, thoroughly spent.

Outside, Sunflower laughed. Eddie said something Natcho couldn't hear. The fire was a diminishing glow beyond the teepee's walls.

Natcho sighed deeply and closed his eyes.

A scream sounded.

Natcho snapped his head up and automatically reached for his revolver, his hand finding only the fur robe beside him.

Again, the man squealed and bellowed like a lung-shot stallion—the voice of pure terror and agony making the hair stand along the back of Natcho's neck.

"What the fuck?" he grunted, rising from the robes and crawling naked to the door flap. He fumbled with the flap's rawhide stays, hearing Keats yelling, "What is it?"

When Natcho finally ripped the flap aside, he poked his head out, blinking.

The fire had died down, but there was enough glow for Natcho to see Crazy Eddie kneeling before his saddle and blanket roll. Eddie was naked except for the burlap cloth tied around his nose. He leaned forward, hands crossed over his lower belly. Blood splattered his chest and dribbled in thin rivers down the insides of his thighs.

Sunflower was hunkered down on her haunches about ten feet in front of him, staring up at him. The girl was naked. Laughing, shoulders jerking, she covered her mouth with one hand while holding a bloody Arkansas toothpick in the other.

Blood stringed from the ugly weapon's curved blade to the dry brown grass below.

Keats knelt on the other side of the log he'd been sitting on earlier. He wore his bullet-torn opera hat and balbriggans, several blankets from his bedroll hanging off his shoulders.

He stared toward Crazy Eddie and the girl, his rifle in his arms, a befuddled, horrified look in his sleep-bleary eyes.

"What the fuck . . . ?" Keats bellowed, lower jaw hanging.

Natcho sprang off his knees.

At the same time, searing pain lanced his back, setting his entire body leaping and quivering. He screamed and swung around, his right elbow slamming against the side of Raven's head as she raised the bloody skinning knife for another stab.

She grunted loudly then mewed like an enraged wildcat as Natcho's blow threw her back into the lodge's purple shadows.

Feeling blood flow from the wound beneath his right shoulder blade, he threw himself headfirst through the door. Eddie screamed again. Natcho caught only a glimpse of the blonde dancing around, wielding the knife as Natcho dove for the pistol in the holster lying in the grass where he'd dropped it earlier.

Labored, animal grunts and thrashing brush rose on his left. He was about to turn that way, when Keats shouted, "Stop!"

Natcho turned back toward the softly glowing fire. Keats was rising, his fat gut jiggling behind his skin-tight balbriggans.

As he cocked his heavy-barreled Spencer and began ambling ahead and left where the girl was screaming and slashing Eddie with the toothpick, a large, bearlike figure appeared from the darkness behind him.

A club rose. It arced downward, the heavy end smashing across the top of Keats's head, pancaking his opera hat. Keats groaned and dropped to his knees, face pinched with agony.

Natcho ran forward and cocked his .45, hesitating a moment as he tried to decide whom to shoot first—the bear-like figure with the club or the girl still dancing around Eddie, screaming, laughing, and slashing.

The sounds of four running feet grew to his left. Raucous growls rose. A shadow flickered.

He wheeled in that direction, swinging the cocked pistol. But before he'd turned full around, the huge, furry, red-eyed creature bounded up from a dead run, throwing itself toward Natcho.

The Mexican triggered the pistol into the air as the beast slammed into his chest, lifting him two feet off the ground and throwing him backward.

"*Ugggaaaahhhh!*" Natcho cried as the air left his lungs in a single rush.

The back of his head hit the ground so hard that his vision blurred. The beast stared down at him, eyes blazing, long nose wrinkled as the hackles rose to show the long, sharp, sickle-like teeth.

The beast jerked his head down, closed his jaws around Natcho's neck, and tore his throat out.

Chapter 12

Camped along the Diamondback River, dozing against a rock with his rifle across his thighs, Longarm snapped his head up. He raised the Winchester and looked around.

He'd heard something.

It came again—a long wolf howl.

The cry died slowly. Then there was only the rush of the river over the rocky bed behind him, and Comanche John's snores around their near-dead fire ahead of Longarm and right.

Longarm remembered the wolf dung John had spied along the trail. He cursed again. Less than fifteen minutes after returning to the trail after John's encounter with the three men he'd fleeced at cards, they'd had to stop because John's horse had thrown a shoe. Stopping had been the best thing. It was growing dark, and John had needed to bathe his cuts and bruises. But Longarm had been impatient to get on the trail of the wolf and the three unshod horses.

The tracks and his own gut feeling told him that he and John were close to Magnusson and his wolf women.

Now he flipped the tarnished lid of his old Ingersoll, tipped the face to the starlight. Only three o'clock. Two hours before false dawn. There was no point in getting started earlier than that, as there wouldn't be enough light to pick up the sign they'd spied earlier—if the horses and wolf were even part of the same group.

He smoked a cheroot and listened for the wolf, hoping to get a sense of the beast's direction from his and John's camp. When he'd smoked half the cigar and the wolf hadn't howled again, he gently ground the coal in the dust beside him and returned the cigar to his shirt pocket. He set the rifle across his knees, hunkered low in his sheepskin, crossed his arms on his chest, and closed his eyes.

He dreamed that he and Cynthia Larimer were coupling on a polished walnut table, the girl writhing beneath him, screaming. But when he opened his eyes, Cynthia's face was that of a grinning wolf, blood dripping from the long, curved teeth.

Then the wolf became Merle Blassingame, and Longarm was running down a long flight of stairs while Merle was shooting at him from the top, the bullets whistling around his ears. Merle was naked except for Longarm's hat, her huge breasts jouncing as she fired her long-barreled .44 while lifting a high, keening, mocking howl.

A wolf's howl . . .

Longarm woke with a start and looked around, his heart thudding. Milky dawn light silhouetted the eastern ridges.

He chuckled at himself.

No wolves or wolf women or crazy mountain men. Just him and John's snores and the cold seeping through his pants and balbriggans and into his legs and butt.

He rose, stretched the stiffness from his limbs, and tramped over to the camp where Comanche John was curled up in his soogan beside the long-dead fire. Longarm prodded the man's hip with his boot toe. "Wake up, John. We're burnin' daylight."

The old man jerked up suddenly, eyes wide and wild. He reached for his rifle and tried to lift it, but Longarm had clamped his left boot over the breech, cementing the gun to the ground.

The old man's crazy eyes found Longarm. They lost their snaky, sleep-soaked glaze, and he grinned, showing the gap where he'd lost a tooth in the previous day's fandango.

"I sure hope those girls don't get you, Longarm," John grated. "I done growed right fond of you."

"That makes two of us, John."

They fixed a hasty breakfast of jerky, biscuits, and coffee, then hit the trail well before sunrise, their breath still puffing before them, the horses well rested and light-footed.

They hadn't ridden far before Longarm, studying the dusty two-track trail beneath the sorrel's hooves, said, "Looks like your poker partners are still headed west, John."

"Maybe they're looking for a digging," John said.

"It'd be just my luck, them shootin' me when you're the one who fleeced 'em at cards."

John winced, his face a mask of cuts, purple bruises, and swollen lips. "Ah, shit, Longarm, I done told you I was sorry about all that. I don't normally go around cheatin' at stud, but I didn't have two coins to rub together, and they plainly weren't rubes. I'd never cheat a rube. I say if you can cheat a seasoned stud player, then, by god, he deserves to be cheated!"

Longarm laughed. "John, I think you'd make a case to St. Pete on behalf of Old Scratch."

John chuckled sheepishly, and then he and Longarm continued in silence, by turns trotting and loping their mounts, trying to make up time for last night's early stop.

They followed the tracks of the threes shod horses up to the roadhouse nestled in the hollow on the right side of the trail, read the note pinned to the door, then continued on past the roadhouse a few more yards before Longarm drew rein once more.

He frowned down at the trail.

"Well, shit," John said, stretching his big torso out away from his saddle as he peered at the ground. "Two unshod ponies."

"They came up out of the riverbank there." Following the unshod hoof tracks with his gaze, Longarm spurred the sorrel forward, then checked it down to a fast walk when he saw where the three shod horses overlaid the tracks of the two unshod ones.

"Think they're ridin' together?" Comanche John asked.

"I'm payin' you for trackin'," Longarm pointed out, keeping one eye skinned on the trail, the other on the brush and rocks and fir-carpeted slopes around them, wary of an ambush.

"All five of 'em had a little powwow back there," John said, lifting his voice above the clomps of their own four mounts. "Now, I'd say the three are hound-doggin' the two, and the two are splittin' ass!" They rode a little farther, John still studying the trail. "They seem to be foggin' at roughly the same pace, judging by the horses' strides."

A few minutes later, the canyon opened out, and then all five sets of tracks swerved off the trail, heading into a side canyon. Longarm and Comanche John had followed the tracks for nearly fifteen minutes, heading past several tapped out mines and abandoned placer diggings, when John reined up suddenly, his dun pitching slightly and giving a frustrated whinny.

"By jupiter, there's wolf prints!"

Longarm had ridden several yards ahead. Now he reined around and booted the sorrel back to John, who was studying a patch of green grass growing among black, mica-flecked rocks.

"Around that spring," John said, nodding his head. "See in the mud there? Wolf tracks. Two of 'em. Plain as a whore in church!" He removed his hat to scrub his forehead with his buckskin sleeve, then pointed with the hat. "See that bent grass comin' out of the aspens yonder? Someone

done rode out of them woods and joined the trail right"—
John swung his head this way and that, raking his lone eye
across the area, then pointed with his hat again—"*there!*"

"Another barefoot horse," Longarm said.

"Shit!" John exclaimed, cackling with delight as he
whipped his ratty sombrero against his thigh. "I think those
three privy rats who cost me my purty smile are about to
git fleeced again . . . if they ain't already!"

Longarm reined the sorrel on a dime and booted it up
trail, jerking the pack animal along behind. The prospect
of putting an end to the evil doings of Magnus Magnusson
and his crazy daughters thrilled him. Besides, if he could
wrap this case up today, he could be back in Denver by the
weekend, before Miss Cynthia Larimer left for points east
again on Monday!

Following the trail, which now included three unshod
horses, three shod ones, and the occasional prints of a large
wolf—a *male* wolf, John proudly insisted—they put nearly
one entire watershed behind them before they cleaved a
narrow, winding canyon. They followed the game trail
along the canyon and a narrow stream for a hundred yards
before a pine-stippled scarp slid away to the right and a
clearing appeared along the right side of the stream.

The clearing was flanked by a rimrock, cedars and stunt
junipers growing from fissures along the steep, stony slope.
A lone cottonwood stood at the far right side of the clearing, its lime green leaves glinting in the brassy noon sunlight. Unseen magpies screeched.

The riders moved their mounts forward, both running
their gazes along the sandy ground by the creek, deep-
gouged with milling horse prints, and along the thin, brown
grass stretching from the edge of the sand to the rimrock.

Longarm gigged his horse up toward the ridge. Thirty
yards from the creek was a large fire ring mounded with
gray ashes, chunks of fire-blackened logs, and bits of rabbit fur. The grass around the fire ring looked as though

brown paint had been splashed in it. In several places, thick, liver-brown gobbets of blood glistened, semi-wet, in the sunlight.

Longarm wrinkled his nose at the coppery stench, holding tight to the reins of his shying horse.

Twenty yards nearer the stone wall, matted grass formed a circle. Small holes had been dug into the ground along the hole's periphery.

"Teepee," said Jack. "Judging by the grass, I'd say it was here about a week. Razed a few hours ago."

Longarm sat up straight in his saddle, casting his gaze back and forth across the clearing, noting the freshly cropped grass where several horses had been staked near the creek; then along the fissured, crenelated stretch of rimrock. At the cottonwood tree in which several magpies perched, crying raucously, his gaze held.

He squinted through breeze-brushed weed tips, his eyes picking out several strange objects lined up at the base of the tree.

He booted the sorrel forward. As he approached, a magpie gave an indignant screech then winged up from the ground—its metallic blue and tar black feathers flashing, a chunk of fresh, red viscera hanging from its beak—and lighted on a stout branch.

Longarm stopped near the tree and peered down, his lips stretching slightly.

Comanche John rode up beside him. The mountain man gave a surprised grunt but didn't say anything. Like Longarm, he just stared at the three men sitting side by side against the cottonwood's bole.

All three were naked except for the one on the far right, who wore a smashed opera hat. Their skin looked obscenely white in the sunshine, the blood from their wounds nearly black in contrast.

The Mexican had had his head nearly ripped off his shoulders when someone or something had torn out his throat. The skinny man had been gutted. The big man with the opera hat appeared to have had his skull crushed. The blood had dribbled down his face in streaks from beneath the battered hat, forming vertical bars down his bearded, heavy-lidded face.

For a bizarre joke, someone had draped the Mexican's left arm around the skinny gent's shoulders, and tipped their heads together. The man with the opera hat had a corn-cob pipe drooping from the right corner of his mouth. His stiffening arms were crossed on his chest, his head tipped back slightly, as though he were putting his face to the sun.

All three sat there as if posing for a photograph.

"Those three—they can't win for losin'," John said without mirth.

Longarm spat to one side, then reined the sorrel around, drawing a deep breath to rid his nose of the death smell.

"Ain't we gonna bury 'em?" John called behind him.

"No time." Longarm rode back out toward the creek and began sweeping the ground with his gaze, trying to pick up Magnusson's trail.

He didn't like leaving the dead—even three dead bushwacking sons of bitches—to the magpies and coyotes, but there would be more dead prospectors if Magnusson and his kill-crazy daughters weren't stopped.

Comanche John remained staring down at the three dead men. He looked up at the birds perched in the branches above, waiting. John returned his gaze to the dead men and shook his head.

"I don't know what Magnusson done to those girls," John said to no one. "But if they did this—and who else woulda done it?—they're eighteen-carrot demons, sure enough."

Longarm and Comanche John followed the tracks of six horses and a wolf up creek from the bivouac, before losing the trail at the rocky confluence of three broad streams. They continued riding straight west through a fold in the pine-carpeted ridges.

Comanche John recollected Magnusson having at least two cabins about ten miles on. He and his daughters were no doubt headed for one or the other.

At around three-thirty that afternoon, the two trackers stopped their horses at the base of a sloping ridge. John uncorked his canteen. "Now we got a decision to make." He took a long drink then slammed the cork back into the canteen with the heel of his hand. "One cabin's that way, the other's that way."

Longarm looked in the directions John had indicated. "Which cabin you think they're most likely headed for?"

"I'd say the one to the southwest, at the mouth of Neversummer Creek. It's the newer one, and Magnus has a digging there."

Longarm chewed his cold cigar, then reached back into his saddlebags. He withdrew a folded wanted dodger and a pencil stub, and handed them across to John. "Draw me a map. I reckon it's time to split up."

When John had sketched the map of the mountains and watersheds and all primary landmarks in a ten-square-mile area, Longarm studied it, folded it, and slipped it into his shirt pocket.

"We'll meet at the base of Ute Peak in two days, with or without news of Magnusson."

John nodded and took another pull from the canteen while his horse dropped its head to crop needle grass.

"If you stumble across them before I do, don't engage 'em, John. Fetch me. I'd hate to have to haul your big carcass all the way to Diamondback."

John laughed. "Don't worry. When it comes to eighteen-carat she-devils and old mountain men shootin' with only half a load, I'm just plumb yalla!"

"These girls are supposedly purty as little red heifer

119

twins in a flowerbed," Longarm said, reining the sorrel left and booting it south along the base of the sloping ridge. "Sure you can resist the temptation?"

"Shit, I don't like to have my haunches spurred by no *normal* gal!" John yelled behind him. "You think I'd let them loco ringtails have a crack at me?"

Chapter 13

An hour later, as the sun dipped behind the western peaks, Longarm jerked back on the sorrel's reins and stared up the steep, pine-carpeted mountain on his left.

He curled his gloved fingers around his Winchester's stock, jutting up from beneath his right thigh, and froze as the sound came again. A low, snorting accompanied by the thrashing of grass and brush.

About fifty yards up the densely forested mountain.

Longarm shucked the Winchester. He swung his right leg over the saddle horn and slipped straight down to the ground. Keeping an eye skinned up slope, feeling as though he were wearing a target over his heart, he quickly tied the sorrel's reins around pine roots curling out of the cutbank at the base of the slope, then looped the pack mule's reins over his saddle horn.

Holding the Winchester in his right hand, he climbed the cutbank and started up the slope, crouching, sweeping the mountain with his eyes. He saw little but the sentinel-straight, deep green pines and the needle-carpeted floor from which they jutted, their crowns nearly blocking out the darkening sky.

The wolflike snorts continued, as did the crunch of grass and brush.

He'd seen only a few tracks in the past couple of miles, mostly of shod mounts and wheel tracks he'd attributed to prospectors. If Magnusson had come this way, he'd done a good job of hiding his sign.

Thirty yards up the mountain, Longarm stopped and stared through scaley red pine columns. About twenty yards ahead and right the pines thinned out, giving way to a snag of rocks and shrubs. The shrub branches were moving as though something were thrashing around on their other side.

Longarm quietly jacked a round into his rifle's breech and moved forward. The snorts and thrashing grew louder. He smelled a wild, gamey scent amid the perfuming pine resin. The hair on the back of his neck stood up.

Something told him Magnusson was near. If the snorts were made by the mountain man's wolf, there would be no doubt.

He moved into the shrubs, swept several branches away with his rifle barrel, and peered through the gap.

His lips formed a small O, and the tendons in the back of his neck drew taut. Not fifteen feet away, a massive grizzly stood on its thick back legs, pulling berries from spindly shrubs growing in the cracks and fissures of a rocky scarp.

Longarm tried to keep his hands from shaking as he slowly . . . ever so slowly . . . withdrew the rifle from the tangle of branches, letting the bows slide slowly back into place.

Shit . . .

He backed away from the shrubs, putting first one foot down, then the other, unconscious of the fact that he was holding his breath. The snorts and snaps continued as before. The bear hadn't sensed him.

After he'd put each foot down four times, holding the

Winchester straight out before him, he turned slowly and began retracing his trail, moving as quickly as he could without snapping twigs and pine needles under his cavalry boots.

Suddenly, when he was halfway down the slope, the snorting grew louder. Brush thrashed violently.

Longarm whipped his head around.

The bear glared at him through the shrubs, the sky's umber light glinting in its dollar-sized brown eyes and in the honey and berry stains basting its snout.

"Oh, shit!"

The bruin loosed an enraged wail and bolted toward Longarm, shaking its head, the thick, cinnamon hair around its neck and hump standing straight up in the air.

Longarm bolted forward, heart turning somersaults as he sprinted down the slope, bulling through branches and leaping occasional rocks and deadfall. He didn't have to turn his head to know the bear was charging. He could hear the enraged bellows and the thunder of breaking branches, feel the ground vibrating under his pounding boots, about forty yards behind.

At the very edge of the forest, his left shin struck a rock half-buried in the loam and pine needles. He flew forward and felt both feet fly up behind him. Losing the rifle, glimpsing it sliding through the grass along the slope ahead of him, he hit the ground on his right shoulder and rolled.

As he rolled, he caught harrowing glimpses of the bear bulling through the trees behind him, snapped branches flying every which way around it.

Longarm dug a boot into the turf, stopping his fall. He lunged to his feet, saw his rifle lying against a tree stump, picked it up, and continued running as the bear broke through the forest behind him and hurled itself downhill like a landslide.

Longarm's horse had spied the bear. Its eyes were

white-ringed as it pulled back on the tied reins, laying its ears flat against its head, curling its tail, and screaming.

The mule had already slipped its lead rope free of the saddlehorn and was buck-kicking and braying in terror as it disappeared through the brush of the incline below the trail.

Longarm leaped over the cutbank and hit the trail flat-footed. He ripped the reins from the tree root with one hand and glanced up slope.

The bear was barreling toward him like five or six beer kegs loosed from a dray, two red eyes gleaming against the dark green forest and its tangled, cinnamon fur. Its bellows rattled Longarm's eardrums. The forest had slowed its descent of the slope, but it was closing fast.

The lawman leaped into the saddle, nearly falling over the other side as the horse lunged sideways from the bank. He nearly dropped his rifle as the horse swung around and lurched down trail, following the long, dry creek bed they'd been following uphill for several miles.

The grizzly's bellows sharpened. Longarm glanced behind as the bear leaped off the bank, lost its footing, and rolled into the creek bed, dust and rocks and pinecones flying up around it.

For a moment, Longarm thought the bear would give up the chase. But the grizzly bounded off its left shoulder and regained the trail in two long strides, its massive flanks jouncing, propelling it forward on its plate-sized front paws, the curved tines of its brown claws chewing up the trail as it ran.

The horse was eating up the ground in a hell-for-leather run. The bear was gaining, growing in the periphery of Longarm's vision like a collapsing mountain wall whirling toward him.

"Fuck!"

The bear came to within ten feet of the horse's bouncing rump—close enough for Longarm to get a good whiff of the fetid hide, see the dust billowing from its curly, matted coat, see the dust caked to its honey-basted snout.

Longarm had a fleeting, bone-chilling vision of the bruin picking through his bloody bones. Then, suddenly, the horse began to gain ground. The bear fell back first ten yards, then twenty, thirty . . .

Longarm's heart lifted. He slid the Winchester into the saddle boot.

He peered forward over the horse's twitching ears and buffeting mane, then cast another glance behind. The bear continued running toward him but was growing smaller with every stride.

The sorrel was outdistancing the beast.

Longarm sighed. His lips curved a grin. He was about to chuckle when, turning forward, he saw the tree hugging the right side of the trail. It was an old, stout, lightning-topped fir. One stubby branch hung low. On the way up the creek bed, Longarm had had to duck under it.

Now he was too late.

The branch smashed into his chest. He heard himself grunt as the branch snapped. The blow punched him back against the horse's ass. He rolled over the tail and hit the ground on his chest with a loud "Ooooffff!"

Head reeling, he glanced up to see the horse fleeing off down the creek bed, stirrups flapping like wings, reins bouncing along the ground. In the opposite direction, the bruin thundered toward him, its bulky body growing larger once more, its head swinging from side to side on its bull neck as it closed to within fifty yards.

Longarm groaned and heaved himself to his feet. His chest ached, his knees and hands were scraped, and his head throbbed from the blow. He bit back the pain and scrambled up the creek bank, pulling at the old roots and chokecherry branches.

Bears couldn't see well. Maybe the bear hadn't spied his tumble, and would continue down creek after the horse.

As Longarm climbed the slope, breathing hard, casting glances at the raging beast behind him, he feebly pondered ways to save himself if the bear didn't take the horse bait. His .44 was in its holster, and if push came to shove, he'd use it on the bruin. But the shots would probably ricochet off its tough hide, enraging the beast further. He'd have to try something else first.

As he ran up the slope, wincing from the pain in his chest and head, he glanced behind him. The bear was lunging, raging up the bank, heading toward him.

Stupid fucking beast! The horse would be tastier than Longarm, and there'd be a whole lot more to eat!

Longarm looked around for a tree to climb, but saw none with any low branches. Besides, the bear could probably shake him out of a tree.

He looked straight up the slope's shoulder, through the towering pines. At the ridgetop jutted a rocky spine with black gaps between the rocks. If he scrambled into those rocks, possibly finding a cave, he might have a chance . . .

He put his head down, scissoring his arms and legs, his thighs complaining against the slope's steep pitch. The skin along his spine crawled. He didn't look back, but from the deafening roar and the thunder of its running feet, he knew the bear was closing.

He stumbled, rolled, picked himself up, and tossed a quick glance behind. The bear loomed like a massive boulder, so close that Longarm could smell the fetid odor of its hide mixed with the berry smell and the sweet honey and dust.

He swerved toward the darkest gap—little more than a slit at the base of the stone wall. The bear's hot breath puffed against the back of his neck, its claws tearing at the sod not six feet behind him. He felt one of the tines slice the back of his vest, and then he lofted himself toward the gap.

He hit the ground on his shoulder and rolled into the

gap, scrambling, kicking off the ground with his boots, tearing at the gravel with his fingers.

He snugged his back to the cave's rear wall, pressing his body flat against the cool, jagged stone.

He looked around quickly. It was a cave, after all. A shallow one. Maybe ten feet deep.

The opening was about three feet wide, but the ceiling angled slightly higher toward the back wall. The bear nearly filled the gap, tearing at the ground with its knife-like claws, snorting and bellowing like a schoolyard bully whose quarry had locked himself in the privy.

Longarm's heart pounded. He'd never known a fear so keen and primal.

The bear dropped to one shoulder and slid its head into the gap, opening its mouth and showing its jagged teeth, bellowing and snarling, blowing its fetid breath. In the dusky darkness, its eyes glowed insanely.

After the bruin had given Longarm a good, long earful of expletive-laced bear-talk, the beast withdrew its head.

"Sorry, you fuckin' demon," Longarm snarled back. "Better luck next time!"

The bruin milled around outside the gap for a few minutes. Longarm thought it was about to leave, but it stayed there, pacing as if pondering the problem of how to snag its quarry from the hole.

Finally, after a good bit of snorting and bellowing, its front paws appeared in the gap, digging and tearing at the ground just outside. Soon, it had a considerable hole dug.

Longarm cursed. The damn thing was going to try and dig its way in.

Longarm hated to make the beast any angrier, but maybe drilling a .45 round into an eye would discourage it. He reached for his revolver. His right hand slapped only leather.

The revolver was gone.

He looked around the lumpy, gravelly floor of the cave, felt around with his hands, finding nothing but gravel and what appeared to be old animal droppings—probably bobcat. He must have lost the Colt in that last fall before he'd dived into the cave.

Fuck.

He looked at the bear. The beast suddenly stopped digging. The paws disappeared. A moment later, the bruin bellowed louder than Longarm had yet heard it. The reverberation made the rock shudder, loosed sand from cracks and pits in the ceiling. Longarm winced at the pain in his ears.

Apparently, the bear had dug away the surface sand and found solid rock.

When the bellowing stopped, muffled thuds rose. The bruin must have been pounding the stone wall above the cave.

"Give it up, buddy," Longarm growled. "I wouldn't be that tasty anyway."

The bear's thrashes and bellows lowered, as if, deciding Longarm were right, the beast had drifted off down the slope. It didn't go far, however. Longarm could hear it down there for a good fifteen, twenty minutes, thrashing around in the trees, clawing at trunks, snorting, and loosing an occasional bellow at the stars that must have begun kindling in the sky above the forest.

Longarm eased forward, crabbed toward the gap, and stuck his head out. Night had fallen, though the sky was still a soft green, several stars flickering through the pine crowns. He couldn't see the bear, but he could still hear him crisscrossing the slope, snorting and grunting.

The bear suddenly fell silent. Longarm frowned, pricking his ears. A splashing sounded—a stream of water hitting a rock or a log.

The damn bear was peeing, christening Longarm his

territory. If he couldn't eat him, then, by god, nobody could.

The snorting continued intermittently for another hour, gradually getting quieter, until the only sounds were the gentle rustle of the breeze through the pine columns and a distant owl hooting.

Longarm waited in the cave another hour, to make sure the bear was really gone and not hiding somewhere, waiting for the rabbit to leave its hole.

Finally, Longarm crawled out of the cave and climbed to his knees, stretching his back, wincing as the skin drew taut against his bruised chest. He was still shaking, hesitant to move very far from his refuge.

Finally, keeping his ears pricked for any sound of the bear, he began moving down the slope. About ten steps away from the gap, he kicked his revolver, picked it up, and slid it into its holster.

Continuing slowly, warily, down the slope, he glanced northeast. "John, I hope you're faring a little better than me so far . . ."

Chapter 14

At the same time, and eight miles as the crow flies northeast of Longarm, Comanche John was looking for a suitable camping spot as the night closed down over the narrow canyon he was threading through low, rocky hills and rimrocks.

He'd been skirting the edge of the Purple Buttes for the past hour. Magnusson's old cabin was somewhere in the Buttes—dug into the side of a bluff, if John remembered right—and he hoped he could find it come daylight.

This had been sheep country since the Basques had first settled here, and several sheep men still ushered their flocks down this way from Wyoming. John had seen no flocks today, but he'd seen the remains of shepherds' camps and what the coyotes had left of a couple of old ewes.

He traced a bend in the low canyon wall, a chill breeze nipping at him, and reined up suddenly. A seep ran out of the sand and gravel to his right, and the final pink glow of the dying sun winked off the water filling what looked like a wolf print.

John climbed heavily down from his saddle, walked

around the front of his horse, and hitched up his buckskins as he crouched, staring down at the seep.

Sure enough. Wolf print.

Big one, too. And fresh.

His blood quickening, he walked around the seep, finding a whole passel of unshod horse prints and the tracks of slender, bare feet and heavy, thick-soled boots. A tomato tin was lodged between two small rocks, where old Magnusson or one his daughters had chucked it no more than three, possibly four hours ago.

They'd stopped here to snack and blow their horses. Then they'd mounted up and continued walking their mounts northwestward along the runout spring.

John mounted up and followed the tracks for only twenty minutes before the night closed down, obliterating the sign. He'd stop for the night, pick up the trail again in the morning. He hoped it would lead him to Magnusson's dugout. When he was sure of the hovel's location, and that the old reprobate and his crazy daughters were there, he'd fetch Longarm.

After seeing the carcasses laid out against the cottonwood tree, John would sooner have danced with a bobcat in the box of a prairie schooner than tangle with Magnusson and his wolf women. Besides, throwing a hitch rope over those three wildcats was Longarm's job.

Leaving the canyon, John set up camp in a narrow ravine at the base of a high, chalky butte. He built a small fire, ate a meager supper, then sat up smoking his pipe, his Spencer repeater leaning against him. Probing the fresh gap in his teeth with his tongue, he smoked and listened to a night chorus of coyotes and hoot owls echoing across the bluffs.

He fell asleep early and was on the trail again at first light, following the trail out of the canyon, over a short prairie then down into a valley nestled in sage-flocked buttes. He followed the horse tracks around a butte shoulder. Wood smoke lazed over the trail ahead, and sucking a startled breath, he drew back suddenly on the dun's reins. Gritting his teeth, he backed the saddle horse and the mule behind the bluff.

In the shade, he tied the animals to cedars protruding from the slope, then shucked his Spencer and plodded, breathing hard, to the top of the bluff. He knelt down behind a domino-shaped, sun-bleached boulder and doffed his hat. He edged a peek around the left side of the boulder, staring into the valley in which a cabin sat, built into the side of another, fawn-colored butte.

A corral of unpeeled pine logs lay between John and the cabin. Inside the corral, several horses and mules milled frenetically, shaking and kicking up dust. One horse was tied to the corral's upper post, and a big, bulky figure in a high-crowned hat was running a curry comb over the horse's right shoulder.

Before the corral, several sets of saddlebags lay amid a dozen or so objects scattered across the ground as though dropped from the sky. John could make out what looked like a couple of coffeepots, a Dutch oven, and hardware including rifles, pistols, and sheathed knives.

Booty from the three unlucky gamblers, no doubt.

A blond woman in a hide dress squatted in the dust and sage amid the bounty, poking and prodding at the articles as if taking inventory.

Even from this distance, John could tell she had quite a figure.

Meanwhile, another woman—Magnusson's Indian princess, with long, jet black hair—was hauling a water bucket up from the gully that ran along the west end of the yard, at the base of brush-covered hills. She wore a man's plaid shirt—the shirt John remembered Natcho had been wearing—and dusty pantaloons reaching to just below her knees. A red bandanna was wrapped around her forehead,

contrasting her raven hair. She was angling toward a bon-
fire burning in a stone ring before the cabin, an iron frame
hanging over it.

Magnusson was bellowing as he worked, though John
couldn't make out what he was saying. He seemed to be
talking to the blonde, but she continued to poke around the
plunder without looking up at him, her tangle of gold
blond hair glistening in the sun's glow.

John's eyes roamed the area for the wolf. It took him
nearly a minute to figure out that the fur stretched atop the
cabin's brush roof was the big, gray beast itself lying on its
side, its head half-hanging over the lip of the roof, just
above the cabin door—sunning itself while it no doubt
kept its ears and nose pricked for interlopers.

John lowered his gaze. The black-haired girl was filling
a corrugated tin tub near the fire with steaming water from
a wooden bucket. Her man's shirt had fallen down one
shoulder, exposing half of one full, brick red breast. John
had been about to pull back behind the hill's brow, but now
he lifted his head slightly higher and slitted his eye.

He should have been fogging the trail after Longarm,
but this could get right interesting . . . as long as he was
downwind of the wolf.

As the girl set the bucket down and began unbuttoning
her shirt, John squinted to see better, but his vision wasn't
as keen as it used to be.

As the girl worked at the shirt's last buttons, John
crawled back below the hill's brow, then rose and scampered down the bluff to the horse and the mule. Chuckling,
he produced his spyglass from his saddlebags, then re-
traced his steps back to the hill's crest, hunkered down behind the boulder, and raised the glass in the wedge of shade
cast by the stone.

The girl had taken off the shirt. She stood sideways to
John's position.

Her silhouette was delectable as she sat on the ground to

remove the pantaloons, her long, raven hair swaying across her dark, slender shoulders, a thick lock tumbling over the breast nearest John.

He swallowed, shaping his grin in his curly, gray beard.

The girl kicked out of the underwear and stood—dusky skin glistening in the sunlight—and stepped into the tub. Her brown-tipped breasts bounced slightly.

She picked up a sponge and dribbled water over her body, then began soaping herself with what looked like a small wedge of lye. When the soap bubbled across every inch of her, like a sheer white gown clinging to her dark, curvaceous frame—she sat down in the tub and drew her knees up.

She sat there for a long time, soaking, her hair hanging straight down the back of the tub, her breasts riding high above the soapy water.

John whistled to himself and tried to swallow the hard knot in his throat.

He was about to lower the spyglass—time to hightail it—when a high-pitched, keening howl rose. Comanche John jerked with a start, then steadied the spyglass and slid it toward the cabin.

On the roof, the wolf was up on all fours, staring toward the shoulder of the low bluff west of the yard, just beyond the gully. The animal's ears and tail were up, its hackles raised.

The girl in the tub glanced at the wolf, then followed its gaze with her own. As the wolf descended the bluff into which the cabin had been carved, Magnus Magnusson ducked through the corral slats and picked up a heavy rifle that had been leaning against an upright post.

At the same time, the blonde scooped a long-barreled revolver from the plunder spread before her and, holding the weapon in both hands, turned westward.

Magnusson walked out toward the trail running along the south edge of the yard. The wolf ran out to join him.

Comanche John could hear the wolf growling and whimpering, its tail cocked.

Comanche John turned the spyglass on the shoulder of the western bluff. After nearly a minute, a rider appeared—a tall man on a cream horse. He wore a high-crowned hat, long, black duster, and stockman's spurred boots. A green neckerchief flopped down his chest. Through the spyglass, he had a long, narrow, sun-scorched face.

His eyes were deep-set, and a brown spade beard hung slack from his chin. An old-model carbine jutted from his saddle boot.

John scowled through the glass, puzzled. Was the visitor someone who knew Magnus, or just a drifter?

If the man didn't know what he was riding into, may the Lord have mercy on his soul . . .

With both hands, his heart quickening, John held the spyglass on the trio at the edge of the yard—Magnusson, the blonde, and the newcomer on the cream horse. The wolf stood between Magnusson and the blonde. The newcomer, facing John and moving his mouth, his voice a low, unintelligible hum from this distance, kept a wary eye on the growling beast.

He cast several interested glances toward the black-haired girl lounging in the tub near the fire. She'd done nothing to cover herself. In fact, she'd sat up a little straighter, exposing her breasts.

The conversation went on for several minutes, Magnusson wrapping a brawny arm around the blonde while the wolf tramped a wide circle around the newcomer, the man's cream mare nickering nervously as it eyed the beast. Finally, the newcomer tipped his hat back off his forehead and leaned on his saddle horn, sliding his gaze between the blonde before him and the black-haired girl who had stretched her long legs over the sides of the tub, letting her toes trail in the dust.

"Shit, don't do it, friend," John growled as he stared through the spyglass.

He'd no sooner said it, however, than the newcomer chuckled, shrugged, lifted his right leg over the saddle horn, and slid straight down to the ground. The duster's skirt dropped around him like bat wings. He flipped Magnusson a couple coins.

Smiling shyly, the blonde moved toward him. While Magnusson took the mare's reins, the newcomer stared appreciatively down at the blonde as he removed his gauntleted gloves and tucked them behind his cartridge belt.

"I'll feed and water your horse," John heard Magnusson say as the burly mountain man led the horse toward the corral. "You can stay for vittles, if you've a mind!"

If the man replied, John couldn't hear what he said. One arm wrapped around the blonde's shoulders, he turned toward the cabin.

John didn't wait to see what happened after that. He lowered the glass, scuttled back down behind the bluff, stood, and fairly ran, slipping and sliding and grabbing small cedars to slow his descent.

He didn't know the newcomer, but what kind of a man could stand by and watch another man walk into an ambush without lifting a hand to help? That son of a bitch Magnusson deserved a bullet between his crazy eyes. If John could put their dear old pa out of commission, how much trouble could the girls be?

Their pretty bodies wouldn't stop lead.

John returned his spyglass to his saddlebags, then mounted the dun. Trailing the pack mule, he rode back the way he'd come for a good two hundred yards, well out of sight and hearing of the cabin, then swung wide of the trail. He cleaved a crease in the hogbacks, riding south then west.

When he figured he was a good hundred or so yards

away from the cabin yard, he tied the horse and the mule at the base of a rocky-topped butte. The smell of wood smoke told him he was where he'd hoped he was—due south of the cabin yard.

He climbed the butte and hunkered down behind the granite dike jutting from its crest. He found a notch in the low rock wall, then doffed his hat, and peered through the notch.

The cabin stood ahead and a little left—about a hundred and twenty yards away. The Spencer was good up to three hundred yards.

John peered around the cabin. The girls and the newcomer were nowhere in sight. Evidently, they'd gone into the dugout.

Magnusson had turned the cream horse into the corral and was unsaddling the mount. John could hear the man's low, self-satisfied whistles. The wolf sat outside the corral gate, head bent back to lick its butt.

Comanche John set the Spencer's sight for a hundred yards, then rammed a shell into the breech and poked the barrel through the notch. He used a small shelf along the left side of the notch for a gun rest and swung the barrel toward the corral and Magnusson's jostling, leather-hatted head behind the unpeeled pine poles.

Drilling a round through Magnusson's head would bring the girls out of the cabin, maybe saving the poor son of a bitch inside.

John steadied the rifle and waited for the man to stand still. When Magnusson had removed the newcomer's saddlebags from the mare's rear, he carried them over to the corral's front fence. As he draped the pouched over the fence, John tightened the slack in his trigger finger.

An enraged shout sounded from the dugout.

Magnusson swung his head toward the shack.

Comanche John's Spencer thundered. The slug slammed into a snubbing post behind Magnusson, blowing up splinters and dust and setting the horses to nickering and a single mule, who'd been standing with its nose to the post, to braying and pitching crazily.

Magnusson jerked his head toward Comanche John, around whose head powder smoke wafted.

John's own gaze was on the cabin as the door opened. A man's hatless head appeared, jerked back inside. The door closed, then jerked open again, and the newcomer bolted outside—naked, shoulders forward, head back. His right arm was bent behind him.

"You fuckin' bitches!" the man bellowed in a pain-taut voice, swinging his head around as if looking for his horse. "You fuckin' cocksuckin' bitches—what'd you do with my *fucking horse!*"

The black-haired girl ran out behind him, holding a knife in one hand. She was wearing her pantaloons, breasts jostling as she slowed to a walk, lips stretched back from her teeth, grinning.

The blonde appeared in the doorway behind her. She leaned against the door frame, naked as the day she was born—a full-breasted, round-hipped, long-legged Viking savage. She had a cigar in her mouth. Blood was splashed across her chest.

"Oh-oh!" the blonde yelled. "Don't let him get *away!*"

The echo of the girl's voice hadn't yet died before the newcomer ran into the trail, heading for the very butte John was perched upon, then stumbled and fell facedown in the dirt.

A second later, the wolf was on him, tearing and snarling.

A bullet pounded the rocks left of the notch John still had his gun angled through. Rock shards sprayed around the opening, several peppering John's face, one crawling down behind his eye patch.

The rifle's roar reached his ears a half second later.

John looked into the yard. Magnusson stood, his open buffalo coat draping his bulky frame, his hat shading his forehead, a big Sharps rifle in his hands. The man lowered the rifle and was thumbing a fresh shell into the chamber when John quickly cocked the Spencer and tried to plant a bead on the crazy mountain man's broad chest.

He fired just as Magnusson wheeled and began shuffling toward the corral, barking curses and bellowing orders at the women.

John's slug blew up dust a good right of Magnusson's right foot.

"Ah, shit!" John rasped, watching the two girls sprint past the snarling, tearing wolf and screaming newcomer, and bolt up the hill, heading toward John.

"Shit, shit, shit!" John castigated himself, throwing his rifle and free arm out for balance as he scampered down the slope toward the horse and the mule.

He could hear the wolf women snarling like female bobcats on the other side of the bluff, closing on him fast.

Chapter 15

John ripped the reins from the cedars and pulled himself into the saddle as the horse sidestepped away from the slope. He tugged on the mule's lead rope and ground his spurs into the dun's flanks.

"*Gee-yaaaa!*"

The horse buck-kicked at the mule, who gave an indignant bray, then bounded off its rear hooves, stretching itself into a thundering gallop. The mule shook its head, balking and braying, and John cursed it and gave the lead rope an enraged tug.

Seconds later, the mule was galloping off the dun's right hip, its panniers bouncing and flapping, the implement handles jerking. One of John's shovels slipped out from behind its rawhide tie and fell with a tinny clank, spooking the mule, who sidestepped slightly, jerking its lead rope taut, before resuming its position off the dun's right flank.

When he'd ridden sixty yards through a fold in the buttes, John jerked a look behind him. Both girls stood at the crest of the butte he'd fired from, staring toward him.

John guffawed and threw up an arm. "You won't be stretchin' this ol' hide, you fucking bitches. No sir! This child's hide's gonna stay right where it is!"

John threw his head back, laughing, as another hill shouldered between him and the staring girls, and he turned the dun slightly into a broad cut between high, pink rimrocks, heading southwest.

He'd probably meet up with Longarm somewhere near Magnusson's second cabin, up near Ute Peak, and bring the lawman back to throw a long loop around those murdering bitches and their plug-headed old man.

John sobered as he headed toward a notch in the sandstone wall looming before him. That poor drifter hadn't seen it coming. Just wanted to wet his stick and ended up getting fileted. Wasn't right.

Just wasn't right . . .

At least John had gotten away. He grunted a wry laugh, relief washing over him. It was close, but he'd slipped out of their clutches, and just by the hair on his ass!

John's mood soured when, forty-five minutes later, he realized the notch he'd been headed for wasn't the pass he'd remembered. It was only a small, inverted V that reached a mere third of the way down the sandstone escarpment looming over him, cliff swallows swarming among the nests they'd built against the sheer stone wall.

In his excitement, he'd headed for the wrong landmark. Peering straight west over the blue green hills flanked by high, snow-tipped peeks, he saw the pass he remembered between two *other* rimrocks a good five miles farther on.

He cursed and reined the dun and the mule back the way he'd come. He'd have to backtrack through these rocky scarps and low mesas for a good mile, then turn west up Neversummer Creek. He was somewhat comforted by the fact that if Magnusson and his wolf women had saddled horses and come after him, they'd still be at least *three* miles away.

Still, John wasted no time heading back through a serpentine crease in the brushy ridges. When he crossed a dry creek bed and threaded a break in the hills, with Neversummer Creek twisting through the tapering prairie a hundred miles north, he halted the dun.

Both animals were blowing hard, sweat-lathered, foam bubbling around their bridle straps and harnesses.

John turned the dun to look back in the direction of Magnusson's shack while the mule stood hanging its head, facing north, its broad belly expanding and contracting as it sucked air into its lungs. John peered across the grassy bowl he was in, toward a couple of near, low ridges spiked with cedars and gnarled pines.

At the same time that his eye picked out three silhouettes perched atop one of those low ridges—three silhouettes clustered so closely together that they appeared one body with three heads—smoke puffed as though from a rifle breech.

As the smoke thinned out in the pine branches, John realized that what he was seeing was Magnusson and his two daughters gathered at the ridge crest. Magnusson knelt behind the black-haired girl, who was down on one knee herself, letting her old man rest the barrel of his big Sharps on her right shoulder.

The blonde stood to one side, feet spread, fists on her hips, tangled hair blowing around her head. The wolf sat up a slight rise and back a ways, tail curled around its right hind leg, staring toward John.

The heavy-caliber slug whistled softly.

The buffalo gun's muffled roar reached John's ears a half second before a searing pain tore through his left side with a jarring *thwapp!*

"Ohhh, you dirty coyotes!" John roared, wincing and jerking back in the saddle as the dun sidestepped. He slapped a hand to the quarter-sized hole in his buckskin tunic, about four inches up from his left hip. *"Fucking dog-eaters!"*

Magnusson crouched over the rifle, probably reloading, as the wolf ripped down the hill toward John. Clutching his

142

side, feeling blood begin to seep between his fingers, fighting nausea, John reined the dun westward and ground his spurs into its ribs.

"Fucking goddamn savage dog-worshippers!" he bellowed, crouched low in the saddle, gritting his teeth against the cold-searing pain that seemed to engulf his entire body.

Another muffled roar sounded at nearly the same time another heavy slug tore up sod about three feet left of the dun's thundering hooves. The mule brayed and jerked at its lead rope. The rope slipped out of John's hand—the same hand clutching his wound—and the mule angled off to the right, the rope bouncing along the brushy turf behind it.

"Good riddance, you yellow bastard! I'm faster without ya, anyways!"

John spat, looked down at his side. Blood welled between the fingers of his left hand. He felt as though a large rat had dug its teeth into his side and wouldn't let go.

He glanced behind, seeing nothing but low, brown rises and occasional brushy cuts. Turning forward, he whipped the lunging dun with his rein ends, angling toward the cut in the rimrocks straight ahead.

There was no doubt they were after him now.

He and the dun had to eat some turf.

John stopped the horse in a high mountain meadow, at the edge of a stream trickling over low, rocky falls through pine woods. He looked behind at the pass he'd just descended.

Nothing moved but the green aspen leaves and a splash of red columbine. The breeze creaked the treetops, and a squirrel chittered angrily.

He'd ridden for over an hour, looking back as he'd crested nearly every rise, and hadn't spied anyone on his trail. Relatively certain that Magnusson and his wolf women had given him up for dead, Comanche John climbed heavily down from the dun, who had already lowered its snout to draw water from the stream.

John cursed, ambled heavy-footed to the edge of the stream, and dropped to his knees. Slowly, he peeled his bloody hand away from the wound. The blood had run down beneath his shirt to soak his right buckskin leg nearly as far down as the knee.

He cursed again, fumbled his Bowie knife from its sheath behind his gun holster, peeled his shirt away from the wound, and poked the pointed tip of the knife through the buckskin. He cut a ragged circle around the bullet hole, exposing nearly half of his flat, pale belly, then dropped the knife in the grass and began cupping water to the wound.

He sucked air through his teeth, squeezing his eye closed, as the cold water bit into the wound, turning his knees to putty.

"Fuckin' no-account coyotes," John rasped, probing the wound with his right index finger, finding the gaping hole.

He reached behind him with his left hand and was glad to find the exit hole. At least the ball wasn't in him, tearing up his innards. He'd been wounded worse, but this one screamed nearly as loud as the Arapaho arrow he'd had to dig out of his shoulder two autumns ago in Kansas.

When he'd thoroughly cleaned the wound, which continued to bleed, though not as fast as before, he gathered a neckerchief full of loam from the streambed and watercress from the woods. He soaked the mixture in the stream, squeezed it together, added whiskey, then pressed the poultice into both the entry and exit wounds. He groaned, squinting his eye shut as the whiskey seared.

When the burn faded, he ripped the sleeves off an old wool shirt, tied them together, then knotted the single length around his belly, covering both wounds.

A half hour after he'd stopped, he took a long drink of water, filled his canteen, glanced behind, and remounted the dun, continuing southwest, heading cross-country toward Magnusson's second cabin and, hopefully, Longarm.

He rode until dark and camped in a valley beside a wide, flat stream looking like pink scales in the twilight. He staked the dun in the thick grass and bluebonnets growing high beneath the aspens, then built a fire, set coffee to boil, and more thoroughly cleaned the wound in the river.

He noticed that his buckskin breeches were bloody all the way down to his right ankle, and he chuckled. So that's why he'd grown so damn weak.

When he'd repacked the wound with fresh mud he'd mixed with whiskey and watercress, and had retied the sleeve around his belly, he sat heavily down by the fire. Leaning against a log, he ate jerky and drank coffee laced with whiskey, then just whiskey.

He slept fitfully, rolled up in his soogan, his head on his saddle. He wished he had his fur robes, but those had been secured to the pack mule with most of his food, his cooking supplies, and his lean-to. With most of his hooch and ammunition, as well, damn that mule . . .

Deep in the night, a chill engulfed him. He had trouble sleeping, he was so cold. His clothes and blankets were drenched with cold sweat. All he could do was keep the fire blazing and hunker down as close to it as he could, his bones and teeth clattering.

He fell into a deep sleep sometime around sunrise. When he finally opened his eye, he wasn't sure what time it was, but the sun quartering over the eastern peaks, silhouetting the tall aspens between it and the camp, radiated the heat of hell itself.

John's clothes were still damp. He felt parboiled inside them.

He flung off the blankets that smelled of smoke and sweat, and rose to his knees. He looked down at his side. The compress over the entry wound was soaked with fresh as well as thick, clotted blood.

Feeling the heat surge through him, John shucked off his clothes. When he was down to only his balbriggans, he tramped through the aspens along a game trail and stepped into the stream, the cold water chilling him, fighting off the infernal heat threatening to melt the hide off his bones.

His bare feet slipping on the slick, round stones of the riverbed, he splashed out to the middle of the shin-high stream and sat down in a pool, his back to a half-submerged boulder, facing the sun.

He stretched his lips back from his teeth as he lifted his chin to the sun, enjoying the warmth on his face as the cold, sliding water soothed his fever-racked body. The water numbed him and the sun put him to sleep.

As if from far away, voices rose above the river's constant chuckle. Hooves clomped and water splashed.

John opened his eyes. A horse appeared sixty yards away, clomping slowly through the water in the middle of the stream—a stocky paint horse moving toward him with two riders on its back.

A dark-haired girl and a blonde.

The wolf trotted along beside the horse, its head down, tongue out, eyes regarding John hungrily.

The girls stared at him, too—a serene expression on the black-haired girl's face, the blonde smiling delightedly over the other girl's right shoulder. They weren't wearing much, and their legs and feet were bare.

John straightened his back and turned toward the bank, where he'd left his rifle. He froze. Magnusson was hunkered down on his haunches a few yards from the water—a big, bearlike figure in his buffalo robe and smoke-stained leather hat. His tiny eyes slitted and his white-streaked, cinnamon beard rose as he grinned his snaggletoothed grin at John.

He was leaning on John's Spencer.

Suddenly, seeing the expression on John's face, he threw his head back and laughed.

John sagged back against the boulder. He turned to the girls approaching on the paint horse, the wolf staying close beside the horse and showing its long, curved teeth to John.

John looked at the girls. The dark-haired girl's eyes met his, and she smiled, the V-neck of her deer-hide vest revealing the deep, clay-colored valley between her bouncing breasts.

John stretched a smile as the girls drew up before him, hair billowing over their shoulders, their damp legs glistening in the sunshine, long knives jutting from scabbards on their thighs.

"Well, shit, I reckon it's my time." John sighed, his eye bright. "But what a way to go!"

Chapter 16

Longarm scraped his thumbnail across a sulfur-tipped match and touched the flame to his cigar. Drawing the smoke deep into his lungs, he sat back against a tree bole and watched the sorrel and the speckle-gray pack mule draw water from the spring bubbling up from mossy stones.

It had taken him nearly two hours the previous night, after the rogue grizzly had finally ambled away, to retrieve the sorrel from a distant meadow cloaked in velvet darkness and shimmering stars, the saddle hanging beneath its belly but otherwise intact, his rifle still snugged in its boot. He hadn't found the mule until this morning, cropping young willows along a creek nestled in a deep gorge.

Longarm was on the trail again by ten-thirty and, following Comanche John's scribbled map, found the second cabin by early afternoon. As he'd expected—because he'd never come across a fresh trail—the taut log structure, perched on a hillside overlooking a small ravine and rolling firs and aspens, had been abandoned, the doors and windows boarded up, a wooden bucket tipped over the chimney pipe, needle grass growing in the adjoining corral and lean-to.

Longarm took another deep drag off the cigar and stared at the rocky twin domes of Ute Peak rising from the pine forest ahead of him, its boulder-strewn slopes and rounded crests stippled with brown boulders and cedars, the trees thicker in the ravines and chutes branching around scarps protruding from its slope like rocky sores.

Ute was the highest peak around, jutting from a pine-choked canyon among other, similar formations a good eight thousand feet above sea level, above the north fork of the Diamondback River twisting at its base.

Longarm couldn't see the river canyon from here, but crossing several steep rises earlier, he'd heard the rapids. Judging by John's map, Magnusson's second cabin lay just over the peak's low, eastern shoulder, near Neversummer Creek.

He hadn't figured on riding that far to meet John. If all had gone well, they should have crossed paths by now, but it looked as though Longarm would have to ford the north fork of the Diamondback and try to pick up John's trail somewhere around the other cabin.

He hoped John hadn't fallen prey to Magnusson's wolf women. John could be nettling and tiresome, but Longarm had grown fond of the old codger, and he'd hate like hell to have to tell the Marshal of Diamondback he'd gotten her uncle killed.

Longarm was trail-weary, fatigued from the thin, high-altitude air, the bear debacle, from having to run down his mounts afoot, and from riding up and down these forested ridges, each one looking all too much like the one before it, not to mention ducking under branches and swerving around deadfall and backtracking after his trail petered out in a box canyon.

With a sigh, he stuck the cheroot in his teeth, stood, brushed off his denims, and reached into his saddlebags for his Maryland rye. He lifted it high, smiled with relief to see that the bottle was three-quarters full, then popped the cork and took a bracing pull.

Enjoying the burn in his throat and the restorative warmth in his belly, he returned the hooch to the pouch, grabbed the sorrel's reins and the pack mule's lead rope, and swung into the leather.

An hour later, he was walking the sorrel along the shoulder of a grassy slope, when the mule nickered. A half second later, the sorrel threw its head up sharply, snorting and twitching its ears.

Longarm drew back on the horse's reins, glanced at the pack mule, which had stopped and was bobbing its head angrily.

"What is it, fellas?"

Longarm peered through the trees carpeting the slope below, at the pines and rocks on the incline to his right. Magpies foraged among the branches, and a golden eagle winged around a granite scarp jutting high above the ridge crest. The only sounds were the birds and the river rapids curving along the base of the mountain on Longarm's left.

Frowning, keeping his ears pricked and dragging his gaze back and forth across the old Basque sheep trail he'd been following from Magnusson's empty cabin, he gigged the sorrel forward. As he moved into the shaded forest, the mule stopped suddenly, snorting loudly, nearly jerking the lead rope from Longarm's hand.

The sorrel whinnied.

"What the—?" Peering downslope, Longarm tensed his back and touched his pistol grips.

Where the forest bled out to a steep, sunlit slope carpeted in brome grass, needle grass, and squaw currant, a young woman was hunkered down on all fours, picking currants from the bushes and dropping them into a large basket of woven yucca blades. She wore no top, and her full, pink-tipped, golden tan breasts swayed as she moved, crawling along the slope's shoulder, plucking berries from the spindly vines.

Fifty yards below her, the rapid-stitched river curved along the base of the mountain.

The sorrel twitched its ears again. As it lifted its head sharply, Longarm leaned forward and, staring at the blonde who had not yet seen him in the forest shadows, closed his gloved left hand across the horse's nostrils, preventing a whinny.

The blonde probably hadn't heard him because of the river's rush below, but the jittery animals appeared ready to pitch and scream.

When the sorrel lowered its head, Longarm removed his right hand from its snout and, touching his revolver's grips once more, pulled his boot from his right stirrup, preparing to dismount. He'd just begun to swing his right leg up toward the horse's rump, when something large appeared in the corner of his right eye.

A tooth-gnashing roar sounded like a locomotive's bellow in Denver's Burlington yards.

Both horses pitched and screamed. Slamming his right boot back into the stirrup and flinging his right hand toward the saddle horn, Longarm whipped his head toward the up slope.

The grizzly stood on its hind legs at the very edge of thick woods and behind a boulder that rose to the bear's broad belly. It could be no other bear but the one he'd already danced with, for there could be no other bear that size—or that cantankerous—in this stretch of forest.

The son of a bitch had followed him. It was stalking him.

As the sorrel screamed again and swung sharply toward the down slope, Longarm's right hand hit the saddlehorn askance. Before he knew it, he was careening off the horse's right shoulder. He hit the ground on his back, the air squeezed from his lungs in a single rush.

He instinctively dug his fingers into the dirt and pine needles carpeting the steep slope, but gravity grabbed him and pitched him down the mountain.

As he turned somersaults through the thin brush of the forest, grunting and groaning, he watched the arrow-straight columns of the pines whip past. His shoulder glanced off one. The blow turned him slightly.

Then he was rolling, limbs akimbo. With each down-turn, he saw the blonde on the sun-splashed slope grow before him. On her hands and knees, she stared up at him, blue eyes wide with shock, breasts dipped toward her berry basket, wild hair framing her chiseled, beautiful face.

She was directly in Longarm's path.

As he rolled toward her, she swerved one way, then the other, her eyes growing larger. Then he slammed into her. She screamed. Berries flew.

She rolled beneath him, then on top of him, and then they got separated for a while before he rolled on top of her once more, feeling her hair in his face, then her naked, sweat-slick right shoulder a half second before his hand swept across a full, round breast.

They separated as they flew off the bank and plunged into the river.

Longarm felt the cold water close over him, his right leg entangled with one of the blonde's. He heard the muffled explosion of a large-caliber rifle.

His back hit the rocky bottom—a dozen hard lumps assaulting him. He got his legs under him and lifted his head from the water as another explosion resounded throughout his skull.

He spit water, shook his head, and opened his eyes. The blonde bobbed up from the pool, gasping and smoothing her hair back from her face, the water cascading down her breasts. Beyond her, a big, bearded man in a buffalo coat and leather hat sat on the riverbank, holding a heavy Sharps rifle in his hands as he stared uphill, grinning.

Up the hill, brush thrashed and deep grunts sounded.

Longarm followed the big man's gaze, his own eyes snapping wide.

The grizzly tumbled down the hill like a huge boulder loosed by a landslide. The bear was heading toward Longarm and the girl, who stood gazing up at the bear, her lips forming a silent "Wooah!"

Longarm's body was sore from toe to scalp, and his brain was addled. He was slow to react. As the bear plunged toward him, dust billowing around the huge, bouncing body, the arms and legs flying every which way, Longarm wheeled and threw himself into the blonde.

They flew ten feet upstream, landing on a shallow bar. A wink later, the bear careened over the cutbank and plunged into the river like a gargantuan cannonball, landing where Longarm and the girl had stood staring up at it.

The splash was like a dynamite detonation. *Ka-booom!*

Longarm and the girl were pelted with sand and pebbles as a wave washed over them. Spitting grit from his lips, Longarm stared at the bear.

It lay on its back, arms and legs spread wide. Blood glistened from two large holes in its chest, webbing like red smoke in the tea-colored water. The bear's nose and toes stuck up from the surface, its brown, shot-glass eyes glazed with death.

Longarm looked at the blonde lying on her side, facing him, her shocked eyes on the bear. Sand streaked her breasts, the water beading on them and reflecting the sunlight like jewels.

Suddenly, he bolted to his knees, brushed his hand across his holster, and spewed water from his lips. The .44 was still there. He palmed it, aimed it first at the blonde, then at the mountain man sitting on the bank and staring appreciatively down at the water-logged grizzly. He held his Sharps across his knees.

"Hold it," Longarm ordered, blinking against the water

still washing down his face from his hair. He thumbed the Colt's hammer back. "Stay where you are—both of you."

The blonde and the big man turned to him dully, as if noticing him for the first time. He could have been a strange bird that had just dropped into their camp without warning.

Longarm glanced around and stepped back to peer over a low ridge behind the big man in the buffalo coat— Magnus Magnusson, without a doubt. Blue camp smoke rose from a notch in the mountain slope, and Longarm spotted a black mule tied with Comanche John's dun gelding and several horses between aspens.

His gut twisted, and his heart hammered. If they had John's mounts, John was most likely dead. Hardening his jaw, Longarm looked around once more.

"Where's the other woman?"

In the corner of his right eye, a shadow moved behind him. A glassy murmur of water . . .

Something hard slammed against the back of Longarm's head. The world pitched. Black balloons danced in his eyes until one balloon grew larger than all the others, filling his vision as his knees buckled.

His gun fell from his slack fingers, and he hit the river with a groan.

Chapter 17

Longarm floated up through deep, gauzy blackness to half-consciousness. He was aware of being wet and riddled with aches and pains, and of lying on a fur of some kind. The fur didn't extend much past his knees, and his boots, when he moved his feet, scraped sand and gravel.

Gradually, he floated up from a sticky slumber and opened his eyes. It was almost like being reborn in another world. Where in the hell was he, and how had he gotten here?

After a few seconds, it all came back—the girl, the bear, the river.

Magnusson.

Instinctively, Longarm's right hand went to his holster, but he wasn't surprised to find it empty, the leather wet and gummy from the river.

He lay staring up at a ragged round piece of sky, a single star winking to life just right of a high, bald mountain peak another thousand feet above him. Around the ragged hole, pale gray rock tapered down to steep walls falling in all directions around him.

He was in a hole of some kind. Possibly an old mine digging. He could see the marks of picks and chisels in the crenelated granite. The opening was a good twenty feet above him.

Somewhere behind him, water trickled. When he moved his left foot, a rat shrieked and scuttled across sand and rock.

Bringing his gaze in closer, Longarm saw that he was lying on a deerskin. There wasn't much else around—just the rock walls and a jumble of stones behind him choking what appeared to be the mine's main shaft.

He turned to his right, and his insides contracted.

A human skeleton lay slumped against a low shelf protruding from the wall—a skeleton clad in a patched plaid shirt, denim trousers, and hobnailed jackboots. Nearby lay a black, knit watch cap, like those favored by miners.

A scorched rock ring lay near the man's boots, humped with old, gray ashes. The skull still had some skin and sinew left on it, but the eye sockets were black and empty. What few teeth the man owned were long, yellow, and crooked. One far back in his mouth shone silver.

Recoiling, his heart pounding, Longarm got up slowly, noting the scrapes on his hands, arms, and knees. His damp shirt was torn in several places, probably by the brambles he'd rolled through. His right knee felt swollen, and that ankle was gimpy.

A tiny man in his head was assaulting his brain plate with a ball-peen hammer. Amid the pain he wondered why he was still alive.

What was the point of throwing him in a pit? What were they saving him for?

Where was Magnusson and those crazy bitches?

In spite of all his aches and pains, he figured he'd live—if he could figure a way out of the pit, that was . . .

Staring up the sheer walls, looking for handholds, he caught a shimmering glow on one side of the opening far above his head. A campfire. The faint scent of burning pine and roasting meat brushed his nose.

He tried to identify the meat.

He grunted. Bear.

Wincing at the pain in his head, he moved along the hole, squinting against the gathering darkness, trying to find a way up the wall. Of course, if there were one, the hombre moldering nearby would no doubt have found it.

Longarm drew a deep breath, fighting back panic as the sheer walls closed around him and the darkening sky quickly filled the opening, like a lid being nailed down on a casket.

He cursed and drew another breath.

Deciding that climbing the walls wasn't an option, he turned to the rocks strewn around the low shaft opening. Kneeling, he removed a few rocks, and stopped. He smelled no fresh air seeping through the tiny gaps between the stones, which meant he'd find no escape route there, either.

Besides, he sensed there were a couple tons of rubble between him and the shaft . . .

"Hello down there!"

The woman's voice echoed flatly.

Longarm jerked around, peered up. A head was silhouetted at the hole's lip.

"Hello?" the female voice echoed again.

Longarm stood. "Get me outta here!"

The girl chuckled. The head disappeared.

For a time, there were scuffing and creaking sounds, and then a rectangular object was lowered over the side of the hole. It descended quickly, the squeaking sounds bespeaking a winch at the top of the pit.

The rectangular contraption slid down the side of the hole to the floor. It was a heavy basket made from willow branches, with a rope secured to each end. The contraption was probably how Magnusson and his wolf women had gotten Longarm into the hole without killing him. Inside the basket someone had piled about ten lengths of split pine logs, a box of matches, some kindling, a folded wool blanket, and a dented plate on which sat a chunk of roasted bear.

Beside the plate, wedged into a corner of the basket, stood Longarm's bottle of Maryland rye and a tin cup.

"If you're expecting a tip, forget it. Why don't I crawl onto the basket, and you pull me outta here?"

The only response was a tug on the rope, shaking the basket. Longarm got the message.

He removed the plate and the bottle, set them aside, then tipped the basket to remove the wood and the blanket. He held onto the basket, reluctant to release his only means out of here.

An irresistible impulse hit him, and he leaped at one of the ropes. He clutched it in both hands and began drawing himself up hand over fist, pulling hard and fast, using his feet to walk himself up the sheer, uneven wall.

His heart pounded as the opening grew. He stared at the girl's head silhouetted against the pale sky, willing her to stay there, to not turn and release the winch.

He grunted and cursed, flailing at the rope, kicking at the wall . . .

The girl laughed.

This was crazy. A sure way to get himself killed.

Longarm's heart beat hopefully as he came to within six feet of the opening. Another four, and he could reach up, grab ahold of the lip . . .

He cast another glance toward the opening. The girl was extending something into the hole. It flashed and barked.

Longarm jerked his head down and stopped climbing as the bullet whistled over his right ear and plunked into the floor of the cavern. Another shot echoed, the bullet spanging off the walls.

"*You fuckin' bitch!*" Longarm grated and began lowering himself back into the hole, glowering up at the girl who kept the pistol aimed at him. He couldn't see her face, but something told him she was smiling.

He leaped the last few feet to the floor of the pit and released the rope. Above, the girl laughed again.

In a husky voice, she said, "You're gonna be *fun!*"

Then the winch squeaked and the basket began rising up the wall.

"So are you, you fuckin' bitch!" Longarm's voice resounded around the chamber, sounding far away beneath the ringing the pistol fire had set up in his ears. "You're gonna be a whole lotta fun when I get my hands around your neck and start *squeezing!*"

That maddening laugh again. The basket disappeared. The winch fell silent.

Then there was only the faraway trickle of water and the hollow sound of the night wind blowing over the lip of the hole.

Wan firelight flickering above, Longarm stood in darkness for a long time, trying to get his rage in check. He'd never felt so frustrated.

Finally, he set to work building a fire in the stone ring, keeping well back from his amigo moldering in the shadows. When the fire was going well, filling the dank cavern with at least as much light as shadow and fighting off the night chill, Longarm sat down on the deer-hide mat and leaned against the wall. He lifted the plate onto his thigh, poured the Maryland rye into his tin cup, corked the bottle, and held the meat to his nose.

Bear, all right. Probably a rump steak. Not bad. It wasn't the Hotel de Paris in Kansas City, but it wasn't bad.

Tomorrow, he'd find a way out of here. To do that, he'd need his strength.

Longarm dug his teeth into the steak and chewed, imagining what he was going to do to those two wolf women and Magnusson.

• • •

Longarm slept, waking a couple times in the first few hours to feed wood to the fire and snuggle down deeper in his blanket.

He wasn't sure how much time had passed before the fire blazed up suddenly. He lifted his head.

Flames leaped several feet in the air. Beside the fire, the blonde stood staring down at him, wrapped in a deerskin blanket. Her greased hair was pulled back from her face and a red-and-white beaded bandanna adorned her forehead.

Her blue eyes glinted like diamonds in the firelight.

Longarm sat up, letting the blanket fall away from his chest. Instinctively, his right hand grabbed a log. His first impulse was to smash her head in. She seemed to read his mind, and her full lips stretched a knowing smile.

Then she let the deerskin fall.

"What the hell . . . ?" Longarm said, fully awake now but not sure he wasn't dreaming.

Her naked body was long and pale in the firelight, the full breasts taunting him, nipples lifting even as he watched. She must have rubbed herself with bear grease. He could smell it. It glistened over every inch of her body.

Standing before him, she placed her hands on her thighs. Slowly, she ran her hands up her hips and across her belly, then cupped the full breasts, lifting them toward her neck until they looked like two round loaves of fresh bread dough. The areolas stretched wide as saucers, the pink nipples jutting.

She groaned as she grinned down at him, the need fairly dripping off of her.

Longarm felt sweat running down his forehead and into his eyebrows.

Slowly, she knelt before him. She reached forward, picked up his hands in her own, and set them on her breasts. She mashed his hands against the heavy orbs, squeezed her eyes closed, and rolled her head back on her shoulders, moving his hands slowly, sighing heavily, and cooing.

Longarm glanced at the wall of the pit. A rope hung down, billowing slightly out from the wall, a couple feet coiled on the floor.

He looked up at the blonde, her neck stretched as her head lolled on her shoulders. He set his jaws and squeezed her breasts. She cried out with ecstasy.

He began sliding his hands up her breasts toward her neck.

There was the sharp, metallic rasp of a rifle being cocked.

The blonde chuckled huskily as he glanced around. The black-haired girl sat on the other side of the pit, cloaked in shadows, her back against the wall, her bare knees raised. A Winchester was propped on her right knee, the barrel aimed at Longarm. In her left hand she held a brown bottle by the neck.

There was a flash of white as the black-haired girl stretched her lips back from her teeth, then lifted the bottle to her mouth, took a long pull.

Longarm curled his lip and lowered his hands. The blonde leaned toward him and, breathing hard, began fumbling with his belt. He shoved her away.

"Get away from me, bitch."

She glared up at him. Then she slapped him—a good swing that bit him deep. His cheek burned. He curled his lip and slapped her back. She grunted as her head swung sharply right, her breasts bouncing.

When she turned back to him, a half smile stretched her lips and challenge percolated in her flashing blue eyes. Longarm slid his eyes slightly to peer over the blonde's right shoulder. The black-haired girl was still smiling.

The blonde's open right hand again flashed toward him. He grabbed it and twisted her arm back slightly. She groaned. Her chest heaved. She leaned forward.

He could feel her hot breath on his chest.

Lust and rage welled in him, and he didn't push her away as she straddled him, pressed her lips to his, and caressed his shoulders and arms through his shirt, grunting and cooing. She opened her mouth, and her tongue stabbed between his lips—hot, wet, and probing. He ran his hands along her bare, firm thighs, the bear grease slick and alluring under his skin.

Apparently feeling his bulging crotch, she smiled as she kissed him, then knelt between his legs and unbuttoned his pants. He still wanted to punch her, hold her down, and strangle her, but at the same time she had such a hard, elemental hold on him that he couldn't resist her.

In fact, as she ripped open his denims, rubbed bear grease from her breasts onto her hand, then applied it to his cock, pumping him and groaning, he wanted her more than he'd ever wanted a woman.

Chapter 18

When the blonde had aroused him to the boiling point, Longarm shucked out of his clothes and pushed her down onto the deerskin mat. He mounted her, and in a few minutes she screamed as he threw his head back and thrust his hips forward, his shaft cleaving her, firing his seed deep within her.

Her knees spread wide, hands around her ankles, she shuddered beneath him.

When he'd finished spasming, he sagged on top of her, pressing his chest against her greased breasts. She cackled and raked her nails across his shoulders, ran her heels up and down the back of his thighs.

He lay there for several minutes, breathing hard, exhausted, before he turned left to see the black-haired girl on one knee beside them, leaning on her rifle. She raked her gaze between Longarm and the blonde, her lips parted slightly, a dark, wanton look in her brown eyes, whiskey on her breath.

Her deerskin vest was open, showing most of both large, amber breasts, the brown nipples jutting. Her soft, deerskin shirt was pulled up nearly to her waist. Her straight, jet black hair hung down over her shoulders, glistening with bear grease.

Longarm stared at the Indian goddess beside him, her deep bosoms rising and falling sharply, and glanced at the rifle in her left hand.

He doubted he could spring from his current position between the blonde's knees to wrestle the Winchester away from her. These women were fast and strong, like Apaches or mountain lions.

But if he could distract her . . .

Longarm returned his gaze to her and lifted one corner of his mouth. "Feelin' left out?"

The blonde reached up and placed her hand on the black-haired girl's thigh. The dark girl reacted instantly, sucking a deep breath through her nose and slitting her eyes. The blonde stroked her thigh for a time, then the dark girl stood, leaned the rifle against the far wall, and returned to the blonde and Longarm.

She handed the bottle to the blonde, who took a long pull, barely reacting to the burn, then offered the bottle to Longarm. He tipped the bottle back, his eyes on the black-haired girl.

She shucked out of the vest, kicked out of her skirt, and knelt where she'd knelt before. She wrapped her arms around Longarm's neck and kissed him hungrily, moving her head and groaning. After a time, she threw her other arm around the blonde and kissed her the same way.

Longarm had been in a similar situation before—once in San Francisco, once in Dodge City. For some reason watching two beautiful naked women kiss and paw each other never ceased to arouse him.

Only he'd never intended to arrest the other girls, or, failing that, kill them.

He hoped these two would get so interested in each other, they'd forget him for a time, and forget about the rifle. But then the black-haired girl pushed Longarm over onto his back. His shaft had been hardening again inside the blonde, and now as he settled back against the deerskin, his cock gave a couple of nods before the head filled out and stood at attention.

The rifle would have to wait, and he felt sheepish for not regretting it.

The black-haired girl climbed on top of him and pressed his shaft against his belly for a time, nuzzling and licking, nibbling his balls. He ran his hands up and down her long, slender back. When she straightened, he kneaded her breasts, working her into a swoon.

The blonde had been watching, propped on an elbow beside them, drinking from the bottle. Now, wanting into the game, she gave an eager, enraptured laugh and straddled Longarm's belly, facing her sister. Before long, the two girls were kissing and caressing each other and nuzzling each other's breasts while the black-haired girl impaled herself on Longarm's rock-hard shaft.

As she rose slowly up and down, her insides like a wet fire, Longarm lifted his hands around the blonde and played with her nipples.

Rapturous groans, grunts, and keening whines echoed off the walls.

Longarm lifted his head to see the blonde's long, slightly curved back before him, her head lolling on her shoulders as he caressed her breasts and her sister nibbled her right ear between long pulls from the whiskey bottle.

Christ. They were going to kill him. He'd never felt so fine about dying.

Giving himself a mental slap, Longarm looked at the rifle. The brass housing flashed in the firelight.

He had to get to it. The only way, however, was to first give these drunk, horny wildcats the time of their lives, so they'd forget all about the long gun leaning against the wall.

An hour passed, then two, and then the spent threesome

165

lay entangled upon the deerskin, a couple of blankets drawn over them. Longarm felt as though he'd been wrestling the rogue grizzly that had followed him over a mountain. He wasn't sure he hadn't sprained something or cracked a couple of ribs.

He lay on his back. The black-haired girl had her head on his chest. She was snoring softly, a little puddle of drool growing just below his left nipple. The blonde was curled up like a baby in the V between his legs, her head snugged up against his crotch, her hair tickling his balls. One arm was draped across his left thigh.

The fire had burned down to a dull, umber glow.

The only way to get himself untangled from these two vixens was to move in inches . . .

Holding his breath, he placed his hands on the ground and began sliding his torso to the right and toward the wall behind him. He'd moved maybe six inches when the black-haired girl stirred suddenly.

Longarm froze, wincing.

The black-haired vixen gave a frumpy sigh, rolled away from him and curled into a ball nearer the fire, pulling a blanket with her and drawing her knees up to her breasts.

Longarm smiled.

Now, for the other one.

Lifting his right leg slowly, he moved straight away from her head, creating a gape between his balls and her curly head.

She sighed, muttered something in her sleep. Propped on his elbows, Longarm stopped. She snorted, swallowed, then adjusted the blanket around her shoulders and nuzzled his left knee.

After a minute, he continued hoisting himself away from her, one slow inch at a time, staring at her, a perpetual wince balling his cheeks, willing her to stay asleep.

She groaned a couple of times, but after ten minutes, Longarm had freed himself of the blonde who lay as she'd been lying between his legs. He turned and, heart thumping wildly, crawled toward the rifle.

He could get to it now even if the wolf women awoke—he'd fight them off with every ounce of strength remaining in his battered carcass—but their yells would no doubt rouse old Magnusson.

Longarm wasn't going anywhere if Magnusson started shooting down at him from above.

He closed on the rifle, reached out with his right hand, and wrapped his fingers around the breech. His heart beat faster.

He was almost there . . .

He removed the Winchester from the wall and, still on his knees and enjoying the feel and weight of the steel in his hands, swung it toward the sleeping beauties.

Only they were no longer sleeping.

The blonde was on her knees, holding her breasts in her hands as she regarded him angrily through a curtain of rumpled hair. The black-haired girl stood before him, swinging the whiskey bottle by its neck. It smashed against Longarm's right temple.

He dropped the rifle, flew back against the wall, and dove into darkness.

When Longarm woke, he lay on the deerskin, blankets drawn up to his chin. He tried to open his eyes but gray light pushing through the hole's opening made his head throb.

Dried blood lay crusted on his forehead. He felt as though he'd been thrown down a steep hill then beaten and fucked half to death by polecats.

Even his cock was sore.

He opened his eyes by degrees, till he could keep the lids open without feeling as though a sharpened axe had been plunged through his brain plate. His breath puffed around his head. Gray ashes smoldered in the fire ring. His

167

bottle of Maryland rye stood propped in a notch at the base of the wall. He reached for it, bit the cork from the bottle lip, and threw back a couple of shots.

Instantly, the liquor warmed him, dulled the sharp throbbing in his skull. He rose, dressed quickly in the bracing morning air, and leaned his back against the wall.

What a rube. He'd let himself get hornswoggled by a couple of women. If this ever got back to Billy Vail, Longarm would no doubt be relegated to stamping envelopes and changing typewriter ribbons for Henry.

After a couple more swigs from the bottle, he started to feel almost human again. Sunlight seeped over the opening's lip, spreading a golden sheen across the floor. Something small and black lay in the dust. Longarm rose and walked over to the chunk of bear meat, picked it up, brushed it off, and took a bite.

Breakfast.

Chewing the cold, stringy meat, he looked up. He hadn't heard anything from above since he'd awakened. The meat had been tossed into the hole a while ago.

Maybe Magnusson and his daughters had lit out from the camp.

Longarm sat back down on the deerskin and ate the meat slowly, taking his time, letting the nourishment seep deeply into him, washing the food down with liberal swigs from his bottle. As he ate and drank, he gave a good bit of thought to his predicament, glancing every now and then at the skeleton grinning at him in the shadows to his right.

If ole Hank or Mike or Pete hadn't been able to get out of here, chances were slim Longarm would. But he had to try.

He studied the wall. It appeared mostly granite, striated with sandstone and clay. Solid in places, not so solid in others.

Longarm tipped the bottle back once more, washing down the last of the meat, then hammered the cork back into the bottle's lip and set it aside. As he did so, he heard what sounded like distant thunder. A single, muffled clap.

It sounded more like a dynamite blast than thunder.

He waited, peering up the hole, ears pricked, listening.

When only silence followed the explosion, he rose and walked around the pit, raking his gaze across the walls. When he found a stretch that seemed to offer the most possibilities for hand- and toeholds, he dug his fingers into a slight crack and pulled himself up with his right hand while digging his left boot toe into a notch.

The notch wasn't much more than a dimple, but it held . . . until he'd almost got his left hand into another crack.

Then the boot slipped. He dropped straight down, hit the floor awkwardly on both feet, and fell on his right hip.

"Shit!"

He felt pressure building. The panic again started closing in. His heart quickened.

He glanced over his shoulder at his pal, Ernie or Hank or Miguel, grinning at him, the long, horsey teeth glowing in the sunlight angling into that corner of the cavern.

With another curse, Longarm heaved himself to his feet, kicked out of his boots, then pulled off his socks. He ran his hands together as he studied the wall, picking out every pit, fissure, bulge, and dimple, plotting a course.

He found a way, tracing the route in his mind. Then, before any misgivings could plant themselves in his brain, he grabbed the first hold, levered himself up, and dug his right toe into a tiny fissure. When he'd planted the left foot along a slight ledge, he reached up, found a solid sandstone thumb, and planted the right foot successfully once more.

Gaining confidence, he dug the first three fingers of his right hand over a granite shelf below a layer of clay.

Up came the left foot. Then the right found a slight gouge.

His heart lightened. He could do it. He'd found a way. As he climbed, he looked up at the opening widening before him.

Then the ram's horn of granite he'd just grabbed with his right hand crumbled like old plaster. He clawed at the wall with his feet and left hand but couldn't gain a purchase.

He slid straight down the wall, tearing skin from his fingertips, hit the floor on his feet, and stumbled away from the wall before tumbling onto his back, the fall's momentum throwing his legs up over his head.

"Unggghhhhahhh!"

He let his legs fall back to the floor.

He squeezed his eyes closed against the billowing dust and the sand sifting down the wall.

A soft whistle in the air over the pit. Something hit his chest.

A familiar man's voice yelled, "Why don't you try a rope this time?"

Longarm opened his eyes. Two heads were silhouetted against the sky at the lip of the hole, staring down at him. On his chest lay the end of the catch rope sagging out from the wall. Longarm pushed himself to his feet and shaded his eyes with one hand, peering up the hole.

"Merle?" he said. "*John?*"

"You all right, Custis?" Merle shouted, staring down at him, her straight blond hair hanging down both shoulders, her olive plainsman hat shading her forehead.

Longarm chuckled.

Comanche John cackled, bearded cheeks stretched back from his gap-toothed grin.

"Don't just stand there gawkin'!" Merle shouted, her voice echoing around the pit. "Tie the rope around your waist before I decide to leave you down there!"

Chapter 19

Longarm donned his socks and boots then wrapped his cartridge belt and empty holster around his waist.

"You ready?" Merle called.

"Just about."

When he'd grabbed his bottle and shoved the neck down into his holster, he wrapped the rope around his waist. "Get me outta here!"

Merle moved away from the pit. From above came a horse's nicker and hoof clomps, and then the slack was taken out of the rope.

Longarm let the rope lift him and swing him against the wall. He planted his heels against the stone, and the rope tugging and jerking as hoof thuds sounded from above, he walked up the side and over the lip, into sunshine and a cool breeze and a vast expanse of sky arching over bald, rocky knobs in all directions. A teepee stood on a nearby flat expanse of gravel, surrounded by junipers, potentilla shrubs, and bristlecone pines. The teepee's scraped hides glowed like a bleached skull in the high-altitude sunshine.

Horses and mules, including Longarm's sorrel, were tied among the bristlecones, near where a spring bubbled up around chalky orange rocks.

Besides the gnarled, low-growing bristlecone pines, no trees grew in the area; only shrubs. They were obviously above the timberline. It was a lunar landscape, the sky scrubbed, the air clear and crisp, the sun painfully bright.

Comanche John stood beside the hole, his saddled dun ground-tied behind him. A heavy band around his waist pushed out his blood-stained buckskin tunic. The right leg of his breeches was bloody down to the knee.

"They didn't kill you, you son of a bitch," Longarm said as he lifted the rope over his head.

Merle rode toward them on a paint horse, the catch rope dallied around her saddle horn.

"Fixed me up swell, they did, then stuck me in a hole over yonder. 'Nother diggin' just like this one. I reckon they decided we had other uses." John laughed and winked at Longarm. He cut the laugh short when Merle's shadow angled over him.

"If you two have had enough fun, we might be able to catch up to 'em. I've been hearing explosions off and on." She jerked a thumb over a burnt orange, mushroom-shaped nob to the northwest. "Seems to be coming from that way."

Longarm remembered the explosion he'd heard earlier. He'd heard a couple more since then, but they'd barely registered, as he'd been in the desperate throes of trying to free himself from the cavern.

"They must have a mine hereabouts," Longarm said, pulling the bottle from his holster.

"They do," John said. "The blonde told me so. That's why they were keepin' us alive. They needed two strong men to work the mine for 'em . . . once we healed."

And in return we'd get our ashes hauled, Longarm did not say aloud. He remembered his dead pit partner. No doubt the poor gent had been forced to help out in the mine till he either got sick or flat-out refused to be enslaved any longer.

Or was fucked to death . . .

"We'll get after 'em as soon as I've regained my wits."
He held the bottle up to Merle. "Drink?"

She reached for the bottle, took a drink, then handed it
back to Longarm. He passed the bottle to Comanche John
but kept his eyes on the marshal of Diamondback.

Merle Blassingame looked fit, if a little trail-dusty, in
her white, pin-striped shirt, red and black vest on which
her marshal's star was pinned, and the black denims art-
fully tracing the long curve of her thighs and stuffed into
her boot tops. Her silver-plated .45 rode high on her right
hip, pearl grips glowing in the air as fresh and clear as
champagne at this high altitude.

"What the hell are you doing here, anyway?" Longarm
asked her. "You're out of your jurisdiction."

"I started losing sleep, worrying that you two idiots
might not be able to resist those crazy wolf women, so I
deputized one of the townsmen and came looking for you.
I thought I was just bein' a flighty female till I found Uncle
John hogtied in that digging yonder." She curled her nose.
"And you trying to crawl up out of your own pit like a
damn crab from a bucket."

Longarm glanced at John.

John shrugged, sheepish. "Wasn't me that raised her."

Longarm grabbed his bottle away from the old mountain man, a sour expression on his face. He felt guilty for
enjoying his deerskin dance with the wolf women. At several times before they'd snuffed his fire with a whiskey bottle, he could have wrung their necks but had chosen not to.

The marshal was right. This hadn't been his best work.
But any man in his situation, even Billy Vail, would have
done the same thing.

He scowled angrily at Merle and grumbled, "Instead of
just sitting there insulting me, why don't you and Uncle
John try to cut their sign while I saddle my sorrel?"

He finished the bottle, tossed it into the brush, cursed,
and tramped off toward the horses.

• • •

"What'd they do to you—those crazy wolf women?" Merle asked Longarm as they followed the trail of three horses around the shoulder of a sun-blasted, rocky bluff.

Longarm bit his cheek and stared straight ahead, fishing for a story.

Picas squeaked and scuttled among the rocks and the short, alpine sedge grasses lining the narrow trail carved by mountain goats. He'd found his revolver, rifle, and saddle in Magnusson's lodge. His hat had hung from a lodgepole.

Stalling, Longarm glanced at Comanche John riding his dun behind them. "What'd they do to *you*, John?"

John removed his corncob pipe from his mouth, spat to one side, then returned the pipe to his teeth with disgust. "Just dressed my wound and let me sleep, goddamnit!" He stared at Longarm, narrowing his eye suspiciously. "*You?*"

Longarm hiked a shoulder and turned around, flushing slightly, letting his glance rake Merle riding to his left. "Same here . . . damnit . . ."

He booted the sorrel ahead and up a bald shoulder. At a narrow shelf, he dismounted and rummaged around in his saddlebags for his field glasses. He clambered up the side of a bluff, twisting around sunburned boulders and stunted shrubs, limping on his skinned and bruised feet, his headache returning as the whiskey wore off.

Near the crest of the bluff, he doffed his hat, then got down and crawled to within a foot of the crest.

As Merle and Comanche John climbed the slope behind him, Longarm glassed the funnel-shaped canyon below him, shielding the lenses with his hands.

On a shelf only about a hundred yards away, and about fifty yards below, stood a small log-and-stone cabin with woven pine branches forming the roof. The front of the shack faced down canyon, away from Longarm. The sun and the high-country winter had weathered it mercilessly.

The logs were cracked and gray, the open shutters hanging askew, the tin chimney pipe jutting crookedly.

The hovel looked all the more stark for nothing but sunburned rocks and boulders lying around it. A wind-battered privy flanked the place. Constructed of slender, vertical pine logs, it leaned in the same direction the bristlecone pines leaned lower and farther down canyon—to the east.

Below the cabin, a mine portal shone in the canyon's right wall—a small, square opening flanked by a framework of peeled pine logs. Above the portal, Ute Mountain reached nearly straight up a good two thousand feet, the ragged, crenelated wall strewn with copper boulders of all shapes and sizes.

Longarm lowered the binoculars. At the mountain's base, and through the naked eye, the portal looked no bigger than a shoe box. Ute Peak cast it nearly entirely in shadow.

Another explosion sounded farther down canyon, the report echoing like a cannon blast. The two horses in the corral off the cabin's far side trotted around frantically, nickering and twitching their ears at the blast.

Longarm turned to Comanche John hunkered down on his left.

"Looks like Magnusson appropriated old Billy and Ralph Bailey's Ute Peak Mine." John scowled. "I hadn't seen hide nor hair of either Billy or Ralph in nearly a year. Now, I reckon I know why . . ."

"Makes me a little sad I came when I did," Merle quipped as she stared through Longarm's field glasses. "A little hard work might have done you boys some good."

Longarm took the glasses away from her. "You're mouthy."

She curled her lip. "I shoot good, too."

"We'll check out the cabin first, then the canyon," Longarm said, ignoring her. "I'm guessing all three are busting rock in the canyon, but I don't want any more surprises."

"Remember the wolf," Comanche John said. "That son of a bitch'll tear your throat out!"

When they'd retrieved their rifles and Longarm had returned his field glasses to his saddlebags, they tramped back up and over the ridge crest, spreading out to approach the cabin from the rear, hopscotching the flat boulders strewn down the bluff to within twenty yards of the privy.

Longarm walked farthest right, intending to check out the privy even though the front door hung open, its leather hinges squeaking faintly in the breeze. Merle walked twenty yards to his right, Comanche John another twenty beyond Merle.

Longarm was halfway between the butte crest and the privy when he heard something that wasn't the privy's squeaking hinges, his own footsteps, or the wind sifting over the hard, dry rocks. He stopped, whistled through his front teeth, and raised his left hand.

Merle stopped suddenly, then whistled to stop John who hadn't heard or seen Longarm's signals. Frozen on separate, wagon-sized boulders, Comanche John and Merle frowned at Longarm, holding their rifles up high across their chests.

The sound came again from the privy. A fart? Or was Longarm's battered head playing tricks on him?

Longarm signaled the other two to stay where they were. He leaped onto the next boulder four feet beyond, landing on the ball of his left foot. He continued forward, holding his rifle in his right hand, approaching the privy's sun- and wind-blistered rear wall. He leaped off the last boulder, stopped ten feet from the privy's left rear corner, and cocked his head to listen.

Hearing only the hinges squawking and the wind creaking the privy's pine frame, he continued forward, moving slowly, stepping lightly, aiming the Winchester straight out from his right hip. He could smell the sewage in the breeze blowing through the gaps between the slender pine poles.

He walked along the privy's left side, stepping into the triangle of shade darkening the stones and red gravel.

A heavy-caliber rifle blasted.

Longarm winced and ducked as the ball carved the air three inches in front of his nose while wood slivers basted the right side of his face and his right shoulder. As the ball barked off a rock to his left, Longarm turned toward the privy, swinging his rifle at the smoking, silver dollar–sized hole blasted through the wall.

Before he could level his rifle, a huge body bolted through the wall. Split pine poles flew in every direction. In a bulky buffalo coat, wool shirt, and leather hat, and shielding his face with one raised arm and his Sharps rifle, Magnus Magnusson slammed into Longarm like a ton of gold ore.

Longarm triggered his rifle into what was left of the privy wall a half second before he hit the ground, Magnusson landing on top of him. The burly mountain man was raging like a lunatic in a blazing asylum, pounding Longarm's face with his forehead. Longarm tried to raise his rifle, but then remembered he'd already fired a shot, and he was in no position to work the cocking mechanism.

When Magnusson rose, grabbed a rock, then raised it with both hands above his head, intending to smash it down on Longarm, the lawman grabbed his pistol from his cross-draw holster, his hand moving automatically.

"Trespassin' on my fuckin' *territory*!" Magnusson roared, spittle flying from his mouth.

As he began slamming the rock toward Longarm's head, Longarm shoved his Colt's barrel into the man's bulging belly and fired. The man screamed like a poleaxed mule. Longarm twisted right as the rock slammed down where his head had been, the big mountain man sprawling on top of it, bellowing into the sand. Smoke and the fetid odor of burning flesh and wool wafted as the ground smothered the fire the shot had started on the man's shirt.

Rifles boomed behind Longarm.

Rolling out from under Magnusson, he turned to his left.

The wolf was bolting toward him from the cabin, snarling, its hackles raised, eyeing Longarm like supper. Merle and Comanche John were firing at the beast, but several boulders impeded their shots, the slugs tearing into the sand and rocks around the wolf's flying paws.

The wolf closed fast. It was within twenty yards when Longarm jacked a fresh shell into his rifle's breech, rose to one knee, and planted a bead on the thick, steel-blue fur of the animal's chest.

Two more slugs, fired from the direction of Comanche John and Merle, kicked up dust and gravel around the wolf's feet. Ignoring the shots, the snarling creature leaped toward Longarm, who squeezed the Winchester's trigger.

The wolf yipped shrilly as the slug slammed its left shoulder. Longarm threw himself right, rose to an elbow, and jacked another round. The wolf, growling and showing its teeth, had pushed off the ground and was wheeling again toward Longarm.

Longarm shot it two more times quickly, once through the middle of its chest, once through its head. The wolf flew back, twisting in the air, and fell in a heap.

Magnusson was still bellowing.

Longarm turned to the mountain man, who knelt holding one hand across his bloody belly while sliding a huge Bowie from his belt sheath. He'd barely gotten the knife raised to throw before Longarm drilled him once between the eyes, the slug jetting through his head to paint the sand behind him bright red.

He sagged straight back, eyes rolling back in his head, and lay still.

Longarm turned toward Merle walking toward him, angling her smoking rifle across her chest while Comanche

John stood atop a boulder, staring cautiously out over the canyon south of the cabin.

"They dead?" Merle asked as she approached, raking her gaze between Magnusson and the bloody wolf.

"No thanks to you," Longarm groused, pushing off his right knee. "I thought you could shoot."

Merle opened her mouth to respond. Comanche John cut her off. "'Nuff snarlin', pups!" John was staring off down canyon. "The wolf women is headin' this way!"

Chapter 20

Thumbing fresh shells into his rifle's loading gate, Longarm ran past the cabin. He stopped at the top of a low rise thirty yards before the shack and stared down canyon.

The wolf women were running toward him—fifty yards away and closing. A pack mule stood behind them, reins hanging, canvas packs bulging with what appeared to be raw ore.

The girls started up the gradual grade toward Longarm, hair bouncing wildly. The black-haired one held a rifle. A silver-plated pistol flashed in her sister's right hand.

The blonde looked up. Spying Longarm and Comanche John crouched atop a boulder to Longarm's left, she grabbed the black-haired girl's arm. They both stopped abruptly, moccasined feet sliding in the talus, hair falling over their shoulders and framing their dusty faces, their eyes glowing savagely.

They stared at him, shifting their eyes to John and Merle moving up from the cabin. Suddenly, the black-haired girl screamed like a she-lion, snapped her Spencer to her shoulder, and fired. The report boomed, echoing around the canyon, the slug whistling over Longarm's shoulder and blowing up rock behind him.

The girls wheeled, hair flying, and started running back the way they'd come. The mule brayed and fled past the mine portal.

"Hold it!" Longarm dropped to one knee and fired three shots at the fleeing girls' pounding feet.

Merle ran up beside him and raised her own Winchester. She snapped off two quick shots, then turned to rake a glowering stare between Comanche John and Longarm. "What—you two can't shoot *women*?"

Merle fired two more shots, the bullets spanging off boulders as the girls sprinted around a bend in the canyon, beyond the mine portal. "Well, I can!" Merle bolted forward, running down the grade after the wolf women.

Longarm glanced at Comanche John, who knelt atop the boulder, his Spencer's barrel resting on his left thigh. John hiked a shoulder and winced guiltily. "My trigger finger wouldn't move."

Longarm cursed, ejected a spent shell, and ran after Merle, leaping rocks and mine tailings strewn from one side of the canyon to the other.

Rifle fire sounded ahead. Thirty yards down canyon and left, Merle was hunkered down behind a boulder. The wolf girls crouched behind an old, wheelless ore wagon ahead of Merle on the other side of the canyon, at the base of a rocky chute in the towering canyon wall.

Longarm ran toward a low, gravel mound in the canyon floor, where potentilla scrub protruded from upthrust rocks. Over the top of the wagon's weathered side panel, the dark-haired girl triggered another shot at Merle. Glimpsing Longarm from the corner of her eye, she swung the rifle toward him.

Smoke puffed around the barrel. Longarm winced as the slug nipped denim and skin from the side of his right knee. He dove forward, hit the ground, and crabbed up to the gravelly knoll, casting a glance through the potentilla scrub at the wagon.

Merle fired from around the boulder, the bullet chewing a divot from the side panel, the concussion making a hollow, wooden bark.

Both the black-haired girl and the blonde ducked out of sight.

Longarm heard Merle curse and fire again, the bullet sparking off the wagon's rusty rear axle.

The black-haired girl fired two more shots toward the Diamondback marshal, both slugs ricocheting off both sides of the long, V-shaped crack in the boulder.

As the black-haired girl swung her rifle toward Longarm, he triggered the Winchester. She grunted and jerked back, then ducked behind the wagon.

The blonde lifted her head above the side panel. Screaming like a witch loosed from hell, she extended the silver-plated pistol toward Longarm and fired, blinking with each shot, gritting her teeth.

The revolver slugs blew up dust a good two feet in front of Longarm's cover.

He and Merle cut loose with their Winchesters at the same time. After three shots, Longarm's rifle clicked empty. He ducked behind the knoll to pluck shells from his cartridge belt and feed them to the Winchester.

Merle fired several more shots; then, her own rifle apparently empty, she ducked back behind the boulder to reload. The black-haired girl swung her rifle toward Longarm, edged the barrel slightly to Longarm's left, and fired.

Behind Longarm, someone yelled, "*Fuck!*"

Longarm turned to see Comanche John clutching his right arm as he hobbled toward the lawman. Wincing and grunting, he dropped to his belly and doffed his hat angrily.

"Fuckin' bitches shot me *again*!"

"Ain't they a caution?"

"Shit, I could shoot 'em now!"

"Keep your head down!"

Longarm was with John. He had had enough. His rifle filled with nine fresh shells, he rammed one into the breech and rose from his heels. He walked toward the wagon levering the Winchester from his right hip, pelting the far side panel with .44 slugs, aiming low enough to blow the brains out of the two cowering wolf women's lovely heads.

They stayed down, out of sight.

Longarm fired his last two shots as he bolted around the end of the wagon, and stopped as he shifted his empty Winchester to his left hand and palmed his Colt with his right.

The girls were gone.

There were only scuff marks in the ground where they'd crouched, shell casings glittering among the rocks and gravel.

A pistol popped, the slug tearing into the rocks off Longarm's right boot. He swung that way and lifted his gaze up a narrow, boulder-strewn trough in the nearly vertical ridge.

The wolf women were climbing the trough, the black-haired girl first, the blonde second. The blonde turned away from Longarm, her smoking Colt in her right hand.

Climbing, using their hands and feet, the two women disappeared around a bend in the trough.

Longarm cursed and reloaded his Winchester as Merle ran up behind him.

"They're climbing the damn mountain," Longarm said, keeping his eyes on the shadow-filled trough.

"Shit," Merle said. "You goin' after—"

Longarm was already bolting up the chute, scrambling over boulders with his rifle in one hand. In less than a minute, his lungs felt like sandpaper. He climbed over one boulder after another, ducking under ledges protruding from both sides of the trough.

His heart raced and his vision swam, his head pounding from the altitude as well as the braining he'd taken the night before.

Fifty yards up the mountain, he tramped around a dog-leg in the widening chute, ducked under a protruding thumb of rock, and looked up. The wolf women were climbing hard, skirts buffeted about their bare legs. There was a blood trail on the rocks. The blonde pulled her sister along by one hand, holding the rifle in the other.

Longarm dropped to a knee. He raised the rifle to his shoulder as the women disappeared around another, larger thumb of granite protruding into the trough.

"Christ!" Merle said, moving up beside him, her chest heaving sharply. "They must be used to this altitude. My lungs feel like raisins!"

Longarm drew a deep breath, wheezing. "I'm givin' up cigars."

"Me, too."

Longarm moved out, grabbing stone outcrops and boulders to pull himself forward and up. The sun reflected off the rocks to sear his face. A cool, dry wind blew straight down the trough, rife with the smell of bear grease.

Longarm stopped suddenly and looked up. The trough was empty, neither girl in sight. His heart beat faster. The smell of bear grease was too strong . . .

The thought hadn't finished sliding through his brain before a keening wail rose. The black-haired girl bolted out from behind a boulder and flung herself down toward Longarm.

A slender knife flashed in her upraised right fist.

From his belt, Longarm angled his rifle up and fired. He jerked back against the trough's jagged right wall as the black-haired girl's shriek rose, breaking on the highest note. She flew past him down trough.

He turned left as she hit the ground ten feet in front of Merle, who'd dropped to one knee, rifle aimed.

The black-haired girl rolled several feet then piled up against a boulder in front of Merle, a neat round hole leaking blood in her forehead, eyes wide and staring sightlessly up at Longarm. At the back of her head, thick, red blood and brain matter stained her hair.

Her face had lost its savageness, her lips' corners lifting slightly, brown eyes soft and lustrous. She looked almost angelic.

"Custis?" Merle shouted.

He ducked as a bullet slammed into the wall behind him, the rifle report resonating like thunder around the trough. Merle fired twice, firing and levering and firing again.

Longarm turned to see both of Merle's shots puff dust at the heels of the blonde climbing up trough then turning sharply left to crouch behind a boulder.

Longarm and Merle fired at the same time, both slugs blasting the rock before the blonde.

"Raven!" the blonde screamed, then snaked her rifle around the boulder.

She fired, cocked, and fired again, then withdrew behind the boulder once more as Longarm and Merle pelted it with .44 rounds. The blonde snaked her rifle around the boulder.

Longarm aimed up trough. When the blonde's head appeared, lips bunched with fury, Longarm snugged his cheek to his rifle stock.

The blonde jerked her head back behind the boulder, and Longarm lifted his own head away from his rifle stock.

The earth shuddered. Suddenly several stones dropped from the wall above him, peppering the trough before his boots. Up trough, a hub-sized rock bounced toward him, followed a second later by several more the same size.

The ground leaped and pitched under Longarm's boots.

He looked up trough again.

Two boulders the size of small wagons were rolling down the chute, as though made of India rubber. The blonde stood, facing them, her rifle in one hand, frozen in terror.

Longarm turned to where Merle crouched behind a box-like boulder in the middle of the chute, holding her rifle in both hands while lifting her gaze up the wall to her right.

Longarm shouted, *"Rockslide!"*

He bolted out from the right wall, angling across the trough and down. He swept Merle up with his right arm and half-carried, half-dragged her toward the opposite wall.

Boulders careened over and behind them. Several fell from the wall above to follow the others down the mountain. The cacophony made Longarm's teeth clack and his eardrums rattle.

Struggling to maintain his footing on the bouncing and heaving bed of the trough, he bolted into an alcove, dropping to his knees and pulling Merle down beside him as rocks flew past like giant hailstones.

As he crouched, tipping his hat against pelting debris, he saw the blonde fly past, hurled like a rag doll among the rocks, tumbling and rolling in a curtain of billowing dust. In seconds, she was gone.

Longarm hunkered down beside Merle, shielding her from the slide and squeezing his eyes closed against the dust. He felt Merle's arms close around his waist, her head press hard against his chest. She shuddered in his arms, but he couldn't tell if she were shaking or being shaken.

The slide continued for several minutes. It stopped gradually, like a late-summer squall, the last few rocks clattering like raindrops on a tin roof.

Silence.

Longarm turned toward the trough. So did Merle, keeping her arms around him. Dust wafted, swept by the breeze down canyon. Except for the dust, the trough looked much as it had before, the debris rearranged.

Longarm looked down at Merle. The first several buttons of her loosely woven blouse were undone, a good bit of cleavage showing behind her lacy chemise.

She looked up at him, then followed his gaze to her breasts. She lowered her arms, pulled away, and, scowling up at him with mock reproof, buttoned her blouse.

Turning back to the trough, she muttered, "Shit . . . close one . . ."

On their way down the dusty corridor, they looked for signs of either wolf woman but found nothing but cracked boulders, strewn talus, and sifting dust. The wolf women had no doubt been pulverized in the slide. They'd be forever part of the canyon.

Longarm took Merle's hand as they made their way over the last few yards of crushed rock and cracked boulders jumbled at the mouth of the trough, virtually sealing the canyon. Dust still wafted, as though a twister had blown through.

Merle looked around. "Uncle John?"

She and Longarm turned down canyon, picking their way among the freshly strewn rubble, blinking against the dust, calling for John.

They both stopped when someone coughed on the other side of a sifting dust cloud.

Longarm said, "John, you son of a bitch. Are you still kicking?"

Comanche John staggered through the dust cloud, his Spencer's barrel resting on his right shoulder. With his left hand, he adjusted his eye patch and ran a dirty finger over his lone eye's dusty lid.

He coughed. "What the *hell* did you two *do* up there?"

Longarm glanced at Merle. He moved forward, clapped Comanche John on the shoulder, then headed up toward the cabin.

"Finished it." He spat dust from his lips. "Let's mosey."